One and the Same

by

I0687593

Theresa Stillwagon

One and the Same

Cover Art by *Angela Anderson*

The Wild Rose Press
PO Box 708
Adams Basin, NY 14410-0706
Visit us at www.thewildrosepress.com

Publishing History
First Champagne Rose Edition, 2008
Print ISBN 1-60154-351-4

Published in the United States of America

A deep bass voice roared, stopping her near the sofa and loosening the beats of her heart into a rapid rush of a thundering waterfall...

She recognized that voice.

"Matt," she whispered. "No!"

He lifted her off her feet and threw her down on the red and green flowered sofa, capturing her hands high up over one of the armrests. She whispered his name again, feeling the heat burning off his body like rays of a tanning bed in the middle of a Seattle rainstorm.

"Matt."

"Kate?" Mint scented breath breezed over her face, sending her heart rate once again dangerously out of control. "Damn it, I could have hurt you."

Jerking up off her melting body, he moved to the nearest lamp and switched it on before twisting around to face her. Nothing showed on his impassive face. "Sit up."

"Matt."

"Get up." Dark eyes glared at her, focusing on the exposed expanse of her tiny middle. "And you might as well cover up, it won't work on me."

"*What* won't work on you?"

"I don't care how sexy you are, how beautiful you look laying there in the dim light, TopNotch Security is not going to finance that damn television show." He glared harder at her. "I don't know what Erin was trying to do, bringing you here, but it won't work. My answer is *still* no."

Dedication

To my husband, Mike,
for accepting my need to write.

Chapter One

If Kate Williams could kick the police officer without ending up in one of the cells, she would do it. "Are you calling me a liar?"

"No, ma'am, I'm just saying I don't believe you've got all the facts."

Kate jerked away from the desk, shocked at the dark-haired officer's comment. "And what other facts would you like me to give you? I've told you all I know. Her neighbors told me she went to visit with her mother on Friday, but when I called her mother this morning Erin wasn't there."

"You admitted you haven't seen her in three years."

"I haven't seen her." Kate brought her hands up and hit the desk in front of the man. "But just because I haven't seen her doesn't mean I haven't kept in touch."

"And she expected you to be here this week?"

"Yes, I've been telling you that for the last fifteen minutes." Frustration jerked her upright and, by the look in his eyes now, she sensed the changed direction of his thoughts. She ignored his stare, glaring at his lust-filled expression. "I'm only saying this one more time before going to your supervisor. Erin and I planned this vacation together three months ago, and only last week she called me to confirm the dates. She told her elderly next door neighbor her mom was ill, and that she was going to visit with her. And now it's nine on Monday morning." Kate dragged in a deep breath. "I want something done to find her."

"And yet no one knew you were coming today?"

Relief eased through her controlled uneasiness when his look moved away from her breasts.

"Not those two busybody old neighbors of hers or her boss and the other teachers at the high school," the cop said.

"Why would she tell them?" Kate pointed in the man's face, leaning tight into the desk. "Those two old women are the sweetest, kindest people I've met in a long time, so quit being so damn condescending."

"Hotchkiss, what's going on here?"

Turning toward the new arrival, Kate held her breath for a moment at the sight of the heart-stopping man who briefly glared at the desk sergeant before turning to look at her. She swallowed around the sudden dryness of her mouth as the towering man moved closer.

Catching her lip between her teeth, she chewed on it while staring through half-closed eyes at the stunning male. He seemed familiar. Something about him, an awareness she couldn't quite understand coursed through her system, yet she knew she'd never met him before. The man looked both imposing and definitely more male than her perception remembered. Strange, she thought. Something about his eyes, the shape of his mouth caught her attention. A shiver raced into her lower abdomen when those disturbing gray, almost black, eyes returned her frank stare.

"Nothing that concerns you, Hunter," the sergeant snapped.

"If this is about Erin Fitzgerald, it concerns me."

Only my imagination, Kate thought with a sigh. He hasn't recognized me.

"You may own half the state but this isn't any of your business."

"I was Erin's friend." He leaned in closer to the desk. "And her unofficial bodyguard."

"Yeah." The two men stared at each other. "I guess you should hear this." She stared from the officer to the newcomer, their dislike for each other prickled the air around her. "This woman claims she's Erin's friend."

"I don't claim it, I am Erin's friend." Twisting back to face the uniformed man, she placed her hands on her hips. "My name is Kate Williams. Erin expected me to arrive today."

"You're Katherine Ad..." the man behind her whispered. Louder, he added in a harsh tone, "You know Erin?"

"Yes."

"Since college, she claims."

Anger widened her eyes, deepening her alto voice an octave lower than normal. Her old acting voice, sexy and sultry, full of promises most men seemed to enjoy. Trying to control the deep tone, she dragged in a long breath. "It's the truth, Sergeant. Why would I lie about it?"

"Yeah, Hotchkiss, why would she lie about that?"

Kate dragged in a deep breath, refusing to look behind her at the overwhelming male. When he moved to her left side, brushing his hand lightly over her upraised arm, she shivered at the warmth of his accidental touch.

Crazy, she thought.

"Well?"

"You tell me, Hunter." The officer pointed a thin hand at her. "You've spent time the last few weeks with Erin, has she ever mentioned...her?"

"She may have mentioned her, once or twice."

"Oh, just forget about it." She dismissed them with a wave of her hand. "If you're not going to do anything to find my friend, I'll just have to do it myself."

"Ma'am."

"Kate." A large hand gentled onto her squared

shoulder, sending a jolt of unexpected heat racing down her left arm. The hand dropped quickly as she glared at it. "Your friend is an adult."

"My friend is missing."

"The police don't normally consider an adult a missing person until a reasonable amount of time has passed," the bigger man said.

"She wouldn't take off without a reason." Jerking away from his disturbing presence, Kate moved toward the large picture window before she turned back to face the two men. "She knew I was coming today."

Empty coldness settled inside her tight body, an aloneness like she'd never felt before. She'd looked forward to her visit with Erin and had become angry and sad when one of the elderly women who lived near her friend told her Erin wasn't home. Erin had promised to discuss the possibly of the two of them doing a television series together. But she was gone. Kate didn't understand why her disappearance left such a void inside her. All she knew was that it did.

"Kate?"

Hunter's warm bass voice sent the loneliness back into the depths of her soul. "Look," she said, "Erin knew I was arriving today. You'll never get me to believe she left on her own. I want something done to find her."

"Hunter, you handle this." Bored with the conversation, the sergeant said, "You probably have all the time in the world to try to soothe a distressed woman."

She followed the second man from the chilled air of the police station into the warmth of the early morning sunshine. A slight breeze lifted her hair, sending the strands flying around her cheeks. She pushed it aside as she glanced around the quiet street. Very little traffic buzzed past her this early in the morning as she walked to her car blocks from the police station. Heat soaked through the loose

4

material of her blouse and skirt, and she relished the feel of the sun warming the length of her long legs. Peacefulness seemed to linger in the air around her, warming the chill of her anxiety.

"Erin told my mother she was expecting a visitor sometimes this week." A rough finger touched her clamped hand with brief warmth, stopping her forward progress. She glanced up at Hunter in surprise. "With my luck, that visitor would be you. Erin's a sly one."

"Your mother?" Ignoring his last mumbling remark, she said, "Erin's neighbor is your mother?"

"Mrs. Hunter, yes." A smile formed around his kissable lips, sending sparks of color into his eyes. He didn't elaborate on what had him mumbling earlier. "I take it you met her."

"Yes." She smiled. "Almost as soon as I drove into Erin's driveway, two women marched up to my rental to see what I was doing there."

"They're harmless."

"I know that now." Suddenly, she realized why he'd seemed so familiar earlier. "You look a lot like your Mom."

He raised his brow. "You can see that?"

"Yes."

His pleased glance warmed over her face, traveling from her hair to her eyes. When his gaze moved down her face to her lips, she inhaled a quick, sharp breath. He jerked away from her and pivoted toward the early morning traffic.

The heat of the morning sun warmed hot over her tingling skin.

"Usually people don't recognize us as mother and son."

"They don't?" She touched his broad back lightly before dropping her hand to her side. "I don't see why not. Your eyes and the upward curve of your mouth are the same as your Mom's."

His finger lifted to trace his bottom lip. "I never

really noticed."

She had an insane urge to place her finger on those glistening lips of his, to trace their sun-warmed shape. "Very nice."

A tight grin formed around that same mouth, moving slow to his darkening eyes. "Yours aren't..." He moved a few more steps into the parking lot. Without looking at her, he stiffened up his back before bringing the conversation to the original one. "Why do you think Erin's in trouble? She probably just took off with that professor friend of hers."

"What?"

"Why did you report Erin's...disappearance to the police?" He looked at her now, his face pulling in tight lines. "She's seeing someone, you know."

Thrown by his announcement, she stood her full height and lifted her head up a dignified notch. "So you think I'm overreacting too."

"I didn't say that, Kate."

"Don't call me Kate." Raising her hand, she continued, "I never gave you permission to call me by my first name."

"Would you prefer I call you *Katherine?*"

"No, I prefer you not call me anything at all." Twisting around on her heel, she stumbled off the edge of the sidewalk onto the street. As she regained her balance, she glared up at him. "Don't you dare help me."

"I wouldn't think of helping you, Katherine."

Stopping at the door of her rental, she placed her hands on the handle and pulled hard before she remembered to push the unlock button on the key chain. She sneaked a glance in his direction. He still wore the same bemused expression. She wanted to knock him on his butt. Why she yearned so badly to do that, she'd try to figure out later. Right now, she needed to get away from the temptation.

"Katherine?"

"No one has called me that in years," she said.

"Your name used to be Katherine, didn't it?"

"What?" Did he recognize her? "It's simply Kate now."

"My name is Matthew Hunter." Bending in a graceful bow as she stared at him, he stood straight again. "And yes, you may call me Matt. I believe you probably know who I am from Erin, *Katherine*."

The urge to ram the car into his solid body nearly blinded her. Opening the door of her vehicle with as much dignity as she could muster, she slid into the plush seat and closed the door.

"I mean it." His sudden appearance crouching next to her window startled a frightened breath from her lungs, tightening her hands on the steering wheel. "It's probably a mistake, but I want you to call me Matt."

Soft and gentle, the tenderness in his voice moved over her like a caressing hand over her bare skin. His voice and the harshness of his words didn't seem to fit together, but she didn't plan on getting to know him well enough to be concerned.

"Kate?"

Striking the sensual feeling from her, she faced him as she rolled down the window. The outdoorsy male scent flowing from him mixed with the scent of the nearby horse ranches and breezed into the space around her, sending a tingling ache low in her belly. She didn't need this now, but maybe she could use it.

"I'll call you Matt on one condition."

He smirked, but didn't move from the spot he'd claimed near her.

"If you help me find Erin."

He seemed disappointed, surprised.

Off-guard, she thought. But why did her request surprise him?

"Look." He leaned closer to her opened window, amazement still widening his dark eyes. As if he'd expected her to say something else completely, she thought. "Your friend isn't in any danger. She's fine."

"She's disappeared."

"You don't understand." He placed a strong hand onto the lower edge of the opened window and leaned closer to her. "I was her bodyguard for the last five weeks. Believe me, she's in no danger."

"Yet she hired you."

"Kate?"

"Matt, answer me this one question." She touched his tightened fingers. but snatched her hand back before the roughness of his skin tempted her to move beyond a friendly touch. "If she wasn't in any danger, why did she need a bodyguard?"

****

On the fifteen-minute drive to Erin's one-story home in the Sycamore Ranch housing development, Kate tried to get Matt Hunter out of her mind. An enigma, she thought, a bodyguard who seemed to be more than a bodyguard. She didn't much care what he was or who he was, she was just glad to be away from him. Yet still his musky scent lingered inside her car as she turned into the housing complex, bringing his maleness back to her mind. She didn't need to think of this man now, or any man, no matter how hard-muscled and powerful he may be; no matter how good he looked in those fitted black suit pants. She needed to concentrate on Erin, on ways to find out what had happened to her. Because, no matter what that police officer and that devastating man told her, her long-time friend wouldn't have taken off on a romantic vacation without letting her know about it. Visiting her mom was one thing; going off on an unscheduled trip was something quite different. Even when they were roommates in their twenties, trying to break into acting together, Erin and Kate had always keep each other aware of their plans. And Erin hadn't changed that much since moving to this small California town.

No, something had happened to her. And if no

one would help her find out what, she would have to do it on her own. Being a licensed attorney in the state of Washington should be good for something in California. And if that failed, she still had her body. Flashing her blue eyes along with a glimpse of a long leg and a pouting smile worked wonders when she was younger, and, from that sergeant's reaction, those ridiculous maneuvers still caused the same response. Kate may not like using her femininity to get results but still a woman used what she had to use.

Turning onto one of the residential streets near a small park, she pulled into the short driveway of the third house on the left. She turned off the engine and slid out of the cool front seat into the hot early June air, quietness greeted her. A slight breeze lifted up her hair, sending it flipping into her face, pressing her blouse and skirt close to her body. When she'd played her break-out character in "Midnight Revenge," she was twenty pounds lighter and fifteen years younger with blonde hair that flowed to her waist. Her youthfulness and beauty gave her the opportunity to play the part of one of the sexiest characters of the year, but it was her acting ability that got her nominated for best actress in a mystery/drama. If she'd only known what that role would cost her down the road, she would have never accepted the part in the first place.

Why are you thinking about this now? Pondering the past reminded her of her decision to discuss the television series with Erin. She wasn't sure she wanted to get back into acting yet. She wasn't even sure she wanted to return to show business at all. But this series was intriguing, with its ordinary people going through ordinary problems. But still the decision was bringing back many unwanted memories.

"Kate, dear."

The tiny woman stood in front of her, a wisp of a

woman not tall enough to be considered a grown-up. "Mrs. Hunter."

"You'll burn that fair skin of yours standing out in this hot sun. This is the worst possible time for you to be outside."

Kate turned, stretching her fingers upwards to push the strands of hair away from her forehead. "It seems all right."

"It's breezy today, but don't let that fool you."

"I'm all right."

A sudden image of the large wide-shouldered Matt brought a groan of pain to her mind. From this tiny woman's womb had come that large man.

"Well, what did the cops say about Erin? Are they going to do anything?"

"No."

"No, and why in the hell not?" The older woman slammed her hands on her hips, standing up straight and tall. Her son's more controlled anger shined in her fierce stance. "Did you tell them about her mother?"

"Why was your son Erin's bodyguard?"

"What?" The older woman looked down at her sandaled feet. "So you met him?"

"He was at the station, yes."

"He told you he was my son."

"Yes, he mentioned you." Smoothing her blouse against her abdomen, she reached down to rearrange her wind-blown skirt around her legs. "Would you like to come inside for a drink or something, Mrs. Hunter? I need to change out of this suit."

"You look very nice."

"It didn't impress that sergeant much." Kate dragged in a long breath. "He couldn't get past...my outer appearance."

The older woman laughed. "Why fight it, Kate? When you've got it, you've got it."

"Well, I don't want it."

"It doesn't matter if you do or don't."

Shaking her head at the woman's disbelieving frown, she dug into her purse for the set of keys Erin mailed her and unlocked the door. The fresh scent of clean linen air freshener mixing with the coolness of the air conditioner met her at the door. Realizing suddenly that part of the heat burning in her skin wasn't from her anger or the hot sun but from a brief touch and a tingling awareness still singing a duet within her, she throw her purse hard into the white sofa. She didn't need this right now, with the mom of the man belonging to that powerful sexuality standing so near.

"He's such a big man," she whispered.

"Are we still talking about my Matt?"

"Yes."

The older woman smiled. "He takes after his father."

"How did you do it?" The question slipped before Kate could stop it. "I mean, how could such a tiny woman give birth to such a…big man?"

"He wasn't always a big man." Mrs. Hunter smiled, the grin brightening in her wide brown eyes. "He was a normal sized child, you know."

Kate grinned. "People must ask you that all the time."

"Or they assume he's adopted." Her brilliant smile lit the entire room. "One woman even suggested the hospital must have switched him with someone else's baby. That still gives me a laugh."

She frowned at the older woman. "That would have pissed me off."

"Oh, for a time it did." Mrs. Hunter flowed past her to the well-equipped kitchen and opened the refrigerator. "Where's that iced tea I made for you last night? I'm parched. Oh, here it is."

"I drank all of yours up this morning, but I made a fresh batch. It's not as strong as yours." She grinned at the bossy older woman. "It should be cold enough by now."

11

"Did you eat? Erin never eats breakfast." Mrs. Hunter looked around the side of the opened door. "By the looks of you, I would bet you don't like breakfast either."

"You'd be wrong." Kate untucked her blouse from her skirt. Still grinning, she stepped out of the kitchen. "I got up early and ate. Ice tea sounds good though."

"Do you mind if Grace has some too?"

"I wondered when she'd show up." She unbuttoned her shirt and left it hanging open as she followed the woman's disappearing figure around the refrigerator door. "Sure, why not? You both seem to know your way around Erin's home so I'll just go and change my clothes. I don't know what I was trying to prove. That damn officer still couldn't get past my...more feminine features."

"You should learn to use it to your advantage, Kate," a disembodied voice sang from the general area of the metal door. "The good Lord gave you that beautiful face and gorgeous body, you know."

"But I'm not Katherine Adams anymore."

Kate didn't wait for her reply, didn't look toward the refrigerator again because she knew what she would see shining out of the woman's features. Disbelief and astonishment, women who've never been judged by anything other than their inner abilities just didn't understand her predicament.

Had this bossy woman's son known who she used to be?

Did it matter to him?

For once she wasn't sure she wanted to know the answer. Matt's presence, his brief caress touched her senses like a balm on an insect sting. For those brief few minutes at the police station, and those even briefer minutes near her car, his nearness had warmed a part of her that had froze solid a long time ago.

No, she wouldn't think of her deceased husband

now. Every time she thought of Bruce, she was reminded of all the experiences they'd missed and it saddened her. He was a good man in his own way even if he wasn't everything she'd wanted him to be.

"Hey, where's Kate?" A loud laughing voice roared through the house like a freight train. "Did she meet Matt at the police station like we wanted?"

"She's in the bedroom, Grace." Mrs. Hunter hushed her with a soft warning. "You need to be quiet."

Only suspicious silence greeted Kate a few minutes later when she returned to the kitchen, quietness filled with its own type of noise.

"Well, there you are." Mrs. Hunter glanced at Grace for a moment before pushing a full glass of iced tea toward one of the empty chairs. "I wondered what was taking you so long. You look cooler."

The jean shorts and bright red top felt comfortable. As she sat in the indicated chair, Kate relaxed against the soft cushion of the sand-colored seat and stretched her arms high over her head.

"It's not fair for a woman your age to look so damned good." Grace patted Kate's exposed stomach. "Back in the day, I used to be something else too."

"Don't let her fool you." Mrs. Hunter reached her own soft hand over and pushed the larger one from her abdomen. "This woman never had a body like yours. Even during her short life as an actress she never played a character like Monica from your first big movie."

"Monica? Damn, but I loved her." Grace laughed, placing both hands on the table. "I always thought you should have gotten that award. Even more so now. You're nothing like her in real life. Not even close."

"I wish other people would realize that."

"That's the price of success," Mrs. Hunter said.

"I don't think your son recognized me."

The sly look that passed between the two older

women brought Grace's earlier comment back to her mind. What were these two up to anyway? Erin had warned her about her two older neighbors and told her to be careful around them.

Matchmaking. Is that why Erin took off because the two had matched her up with someone she didn't care for, and he wouldn't accept no for an answer? Like that man who'd stalked her. No, the two ladies wouldn't match her up with someone that evil. So why *did* she leave?

Maybe Matt's implied romantic interlude wasn't as far fetched as she thought. Maybe Erin left with someone she'd fallen in love with like that professor friend of hers.

Oh, Erin, where are you anyway?

****

The building stood at the end of a long dusty street, looking much as it had when Matt first been there with his uncle twenty years ago. A low, one-story structure painted gray and white. The only difference was the large square sign leaning against the side wall, with the letters facing inward. The first thing Matt did was take the sign down and put up the new one: TopNotch Security, Inc.

"Hey, Matt." Carlos Lopez, Matt's friend and partner, looked to him. "Are you gong to stare at that building all day, or what?"

"It doesn't look much different than it did years ago."

Carlos nodded. "The previous owners kept it up, that's for sure."

He twisted back to glance at the familiar building, grinning in memory of a time long gone. "My uncle was so proud when he purchased this place, the beginning of TopNotch Security."

"And now it again belongs to TopNotch."

"He should've never sold it," Matt said, "He should never have moved the headquarters to San Diego."

"I talked to that police officer about starting a neighborhood watch program." Matt spun back to stare at the small Hispanic man before entering the building. He led Carlos past the dingy front area to the small office at the back of the long room. "He seemed interested."

"Si," Carlos agreed, "It'll be nice to get back to the basics again."

Matt settled his long body into the chair behind the desk; Carlos sank into the other one. "Yes."

A sharp slap hit against the dusty surface between them, pulling Matt out of his planning, "Oh, I meant to ask...did you find out anything about Erin?"

"No." Blonde hair sweeping soft over a smooth oval face with wide sky-blue eyes rose so suddenly into his mind he leaned back into his chair. Firm breasts, a tiny waist and the longest legs he'd ever seen completed the picture. Man, but Katherine Adams still looked good, even better than she did ten years ago when she was at the top of her game. "But I know now why my mother decided to send me to the police station today. She didn't tell me Erin's friend would be there. I should've realized something was up when Erin started telling me about her relationship with Kate."

"Kate?"

"Kate Williams."

"Who's Kate Williams?"

Only the sexiest lady in the galaxy, he thought. But he said, "Maybe the name Katherine Adams will sound more familiar to you."

"Katherine Adams?" Carlos looked out the single window before shaking his head. "Sorry, that name doesn't ring a bell. Is she one of our clients? Does she work with one of our clients?"

"If Erin has her way, she will be one soon," he muttered. "In a way."

"Or is she one of your...ladies?"

The image of her standing tall and straight profiled in full exposure as she yelled at that police officer earlier this morning made him smile. He'd recognized her right away. She may have changed her name but there was no changing that face—or body.

"Matt, do you need me to clean up another one of your messes?"

"What?" He pushed the image from his mind and concentrated on his friend. "Oh, it's nothing like that. Kate and I...never met until this morning."

But Katherine he knew well. At least as well as any obsessed fan knew someone, and he was glad Carlos didn't remember their college years. He would never hear the end of it.

"I was hoping it was a woman." His friend stared hard at him. "I was hoping you've gotten back into circulation. Man, how long has it been? I've never known you to go without sex for so long. You must be hurting bad."

"I've other things to think about now." Matt leaned in the chair. "It'll be good to start moving our headquarters here."

"No really, how long has it been?" Carlos ignored his attempt at changing the subject. "Four months? Five? Man, I can't go a week without grabbing my gorgeous wife."

"Six," he said, "and I feel fine."

"That's a long time for a babe magnet like you to go without sex. I think you're losing your touch with the ladies."

"You haven't called me that since college."

"But I've always thought it," Carlos said. "I don't know what's happening to you, man. That Anna babe musta messed you up so bad you've given up on women altogether."

He didn't want to think of Anna. She'd been his whole life, promising him forever. She'd promised him marriage and children, but he'd only gotten six months and an empty house. He'd thought she'd cared about him, wanted to be his wife, but all along—

"Man, I'm sorry I brought her up." The smaller man tilted his head back, cradling his arms behind it. "So this Kate woman, is she a looker?"

"Kate?"

"She must be for you to be so preoccupied." Carlos stretched his legs on the scarred desk, crossing his ankles. "I mean, she must be something because you didn't react to me putting my feet up on this desk."

"Your shoes won't hurt this old thing, Carlos." He tapped the wood hard with his knuckles before getting up from his chair and walking to the only window in the cramped room. Outdoors, a view of the side alleyway greeted his unfocused gaze. "I wish I was thinking about Anna. It'll be easier for me."

"You do?"

"I wonder where that contractor we hired is," Matt said lightly. "He should be here by now."

"Settle down, man." Carlos lifted a hand and rubbed the top of his balding head. "You'll just have to be a little patient."

"I'll be glad to get this out of the way." He placed his hand on the window, chilled air from the air conditioner mixed with the heat radiating from the sun to warm his palm. "I'm looking forward to getting back to San Diego, to start planning the move."

"Mary and I are thinking of starting a family."

He turned at Carlos' abrupt change of subject and smiled. "So Mary likes it here, does she?"

"She says it's peaceful." Carlos glanced toward the window and grinned back. "I think I might like becoming a daddy now. This town seems like a nice place to raise children. Mary wants a couple."

"Yeah, this is a great place to grow up." Matt leaned into the window frame and crossed his arms at his waist. "The town has a lot of elderly people but it's safe and small enough to raise children."

"Then why are you in such a hurry to leave," Carlos asked. "We have people who can take care of the move in San Diego. You don't need to get involved."

"I'm...not really sure."

A knock sounded on the door at the same time Carlos jerked his feet from the desk and slammed them hard onto the floor. Eyes bright, grin wide in his narrow face, Carlos said, "Oh, I just remembered Katherine Adams. Wow."

"Just answer the door, Lopez."

He grinned. "This is only a delay of our discussion, man."

Matt shook his head before settling down behind the old desk. "Just let the man in."

Chapter Two

An hour after the two women left the house; Kate dug in her heels and stretched her legs while pushing the office chair away from the desk. She read her last e-mail from her assistant and decided to give her eyes a rest. It was always amazing how much correspondence a partner in a law firm received on any given day. An hour squinting at a small laptop screen should be enough time to finish catching up with her office in Seattle.

She stretched her arms in the air before rolling her chair back to the laptop and typing one last note. Martin, the newest partner in the firm, was a brilliant lawyer, but she didn't believe his heart was in this particular case because it wasn't a high profile one.

Sometimes all her partners bugged her. If they didn't have a chance of earning a huge sum of money from a settlement, they didn't want to give their all to that particular client.

Bruce had been like that too.

Beep. "Mail truck," sounded in the air as she sent her last e-mail. She decided to check the new message before logging off.

Kate,

Hi, how are you doing? Sorry I wasn't there to greet you at your arrival on Saturday. Something important came up and I couldn't reach you until now. What time is it there anyway? Noon? One? I'm confused about the time changes. Oh, well—I told Esther and Grace that my mom was sick, but I guess by now you know that was a bit of a lie. Don't worry,

I'm fine.

Well actually I'm more than fine. I'm married, but don't tell anyone. I'll explain everything when I return. I'll call you at my place, on my phone in a few days, so don't you dare go anywhere. I'll be back by next week. Hopefully. I've missed you.

So have you been giving much thought to doing the series? Have you found the time to read the script yet? I think you'll like it.

Oh, and have you met my neighbor's gorgeous son? Hot stuff, isn't he?

See you in a week or so,

Erin

"Married? Why you little—" Kate whispered as she hit reply to sender. "Now you tell me."

After she'd made such a fool of herself this morning in front of that police officer and the aforementioned sexy male.

And why was she asking about that man, anyway?

Kate typed.

Erin,

So who is the lucky guy? Don't worry your secret is safe.

I'm glad to hear you're all right. I wish you would've emailed me yesterday before I went to the police station. I was about ready to go searching for you myself.

No, I haven't had a chance to read the script.

And why are you asking about your neighbor's son? I'm not interested.

I was worried about you.

Kate

As she sent the email, turned off the computer and cleared the desk, the last few sentences of Erin's message crossed her mind. Why would she ask either question? How could she decide on doing the television pilot for "Three Sisters" until they'd talked? And why in the world would she ask if she'd met Matt?

A mystery, maybe. She hated mysteries.

Kate shook her head and wandered into the bedroom to change into a one-piece light green bathing suit, grabbed up a bottle of suntan lotion as she raced out the door to the pool. Kate opened the bottle and poured it into her hands, rubbing the SPC 30 lotion all over her exposed skin.

"Ah." Yes, this was what she needed right now. Lying back on the lounger, she deposited the lotion bottle on the ground beside her and closed her eyes. Her legs stretched out long on the chaise and arms curving up and over her head, she inhaled a cleansing breath of fresh air. The warmth from the sun penetrated her chilled body, heating the outside of her light Seattle skin with piercing rays.

It felt like heaven. She grinned, stretching her arms up higher over her head and dropping them to her sides on the lounger.

Wasn't hell supposed to be the hot place?

"Ms. Fitzgerald."

A high-pitched male voice sounded in her half-sleep, jerking her up and out of the chair. Her bare toe stumbled over a sharp stone, causing her to leap away from the lounger. A soft swear word issued from deep inside her.

"Ma'am, I'm sorry." The young man tried to hide his laughter, but his large beaming smile showed it clear to her. "I was looking for Ms. Fitzgerald."

Kate lifted her foot a few inches from the ground and glanced at her toe before sitting back on the chaise. "It looks okay."

"Ms. Fitzgerald lets us come visit her," he added.

"Where is she?" A second voice demanded from behind the tall awkward boy. A cute, bit overweight girl peeked around his side. "She promised to be the advisor for our play at the playhouse."

"She did?"

"Yes, ma'am."

This boy made her feel ancient with his use of the polite term. I'm only thirty-seven, she wanted to tell him. But wouldn't that be ancient to a high school kid?

"She promised us in English class at the end of the year. Is she here?" the boy asked.

"I'm sorry to say she's not."

"I knew she wouldn't do it." The girl stomped her foot on the ground and wrapped her arms tight around her middle. "She's too busy to help out a bunch of kids like us."

"Why don't you just quit complaining?" His harsh words clamped the girl's mouth shut. "Ms. Fitzgerald's not like that at all."

Kate wanted to tell the boy it was rude of him to yell at his friend, but the girl's glare stopped her.

"Where is she, ma'am?"

"I'm not sure." She reached down to pick up her wrap, staring back at the now silent boy. His eyes angled downward when he noticed her perusal, a flushed look of sweet innocence reddening his tanned skin. She smiled. Old men and young boys were safe; not like that man at the police station at all. "She just sent me an e-mail, but she didn't say where she was or when she'd be back. Sorry."

"She's supposed to be our advisor this year," whispered the girl. "She promised."

"She promised you that?" Maybe I could help the kids, Kate thought. Maybe she could be a substitute for Erin. It would keep her busy until Erin returned from...wherever. "What play do you plan on doing?"

The boy ignored her question for two of his own. "Why did Ms. Fitzgerald leave town right now? Is she on vacation?"

"She didn't say." Kate glanced at the girl for a moment before focusing on the more ongoing boy. "Do you think I could help?"

"You?" Disbelief sounded in the girl's voice now. "Who are you anyway? Are you a teacher too?"

Kate smiled at the young girl's words. Didn't they know who Erin was in her former life? Didn't they know that, less than fifteen years ago, she was one of the most sought after young actresses? "No, but I do know a bit about acting and directing. I'm involved with a small theater group in Seattle. Maybe I could be of help to you until Erin returns."

"Have you been friend's for a long time?" the boy asked.

"Yes." Grinning at the boy's bright glance, she added, "The two of you weren't even born when we first met."

"Probably not, ma'am." A silly grin lifted up the boy's tight frown, a smile that showed clear in his wide-opened eyes. "You are pretty old."

This kid was going to be a looker when he filled out some, and after his voice changed. "You think I'm old?" Raising her hand up to point at them, she glanced beyond the boy to stare at the pouting girl behind him. "I'll have you both know I am only thirty-seven years old."

"Thirty-seven?" The girl's grin matched the boy's and she suddenly saw the similarity between the two. The same sparkling green eyes and dark blonde hair, the same physical shape of their heads and movements told her these two were more than just friends. "Our math teacher just turned thirty and she says she's old."

"Age is all in your head."

"Isn't that what all old people say?" The boy glanced back at the girl and grinned. "It's a way for them to stay young."

The girl laughed and nodded at the boy's joke. Oh, yeah, Kate thought, I'm going to like working with these siblings. If they'd let her help them out with the show, it would be great. She would love to get involved with the production in some small way.

"You know, Sis, maybe this lady could help." He turned to face her. "If you really want to, I guess you'll do."

"I would love to help." Kate glanced at their dark tanned skin. "If I don't get out of this sun, I'm going to burn."

"Yeah, you are a bit white."

"She looks a little pink to me," his sister added, "I didn't know anyone could be that pale."

Why she wanted to help these two she'd never know?

****

Matt slammed the blueprints on the bed and scrubbed his hands over his dry eyes. Hand written notes filled with questions and possible changes littered the neatly made bed. When he'd returned this afternoon from the worksite, the room had been sparkling clean and fresh like hotel rooms across the country. Now it looked like an earthquake had hit, Matt shook his head at the thought, grinning softly. A knock sounding on the door brought his head up. "It's unlocked."

"Hey, man."

"Carlos."

His partner wandered into the room and looked around at the messy area. "You used to be such a neat person."

"I know." Matt grinned and added, "And it always bugged you."

"It's not normal."

Carlos pulled Matt's notebook from beneath the crumbled blueprint and sat down in the chair beside the desk, throwing a bunch of computer printouts on the bed. "Those are the records you wanted me to get for you. I printed out only the basic information for each employee. Hotchkiss finally gave me the password to the employee database."

"Good."

"He's a fierce guy, man."

"I've noticed." Matt picked up the top folder and glanced at it before setting it back down. "I'm glad he decided to cooperate with us. TopNotch owns this business now, but I didn't want to cause any trouble in my mom's hometown." When Carlos didn't answer, he asked, "What so interesting over there? If Mary finds out you're looking at naked ladies again, she'll—"

"Screw you, Hunter."

As the silence lingered, Matt picked up the top folder once again and opened it. The personnel file of one of older workers he'd promised to keep in his employ.

"Hey, did you ever decide on that series deal?" Carlos asked.

A hard ached pierced him. "What?"

"You know, the one Erin tried to talk you into a few months ago." He glanced up from the computer screen and stared at Matt. "If I remember correctly, I thought it was a good idea, but you were still too pissed off at what Anna did to you to even consider it."

"I'm still not going to consider it."

"Then why did the writer send you a copy of the script?"

Matt sat in frozen silence, as page after page appeared in his printer's tray. No words came to mind as he watched his friend gather up the pages and pile them together on the desk.

"Someone must have gotten the wrong idea," Carlos added.

"Damn, I should've known she was here for more than a visit with her friend."

"Hey, don't start jumping to conclusions."

Matt leaped from the bed and raced to the window. He fisted his hands together in a futile attempt to calm his temper. "Why else would she be here, now? Kate hasn't seen Erin in three years. Now, all of a sudden, she shows up. Don't you think it's a little suspicious?"

"Erin told you she was coming to discuss the

series, didn't she?"

Carlos spoke the truth, yet he didn't want to hear it. All he saw was Anna's disappointed anger when he'd told her no. Two totally different things, two totally different people, yet still—

"Kate's not hiding the facts about the series."

"She mentioned some business she had to discuss with Erin." Matt glanced quickly at him. "But she didn't say what it was."

His friend looked at him with an intense gaze for a long time, seeing everything Matt tried to hide. "You can't judge every woman's motivation by Anna's. Give the lady a chance, why don't you?"

While he mulled over Carlos' words, the cell phone on the bed stand rang and he picked it up like a lifeline. "Hunter speaking."

"Boy, this is your Aunt Grace."

"Grace, what's wrong?"

"It's your...mom." Trembling words, harsh indwelled breath spoke her fear. "I think...someone's sneaking around her house. Matt, I thought I saw someone stalking around the front yard. It's nine at night. Your mom's always in bed by this time." After a moment, she added, "You need to get there now."

"Call the police, Aunt Grace, I'm on the way."

Carlos stood close to him when he hung up the phone, and he welcomed his friend's tightened grip on his shoulder. "Is she all right?"

"I need to get to her house."

"Do you want me to do anything from here?"

"No, she is calling the police." He handed his friend the cell phone and turned toward the hotel room door. "I'll let you know what's going on—"

"Go, Matt." Lifting the phone, Carlos said, "I'll keep this thing near me until you call. I hope everything turns out okay."

"It has to be." Matt swallowed hard, fighting down the need to rush into the darkening night. "It has to be."

****

A sound woke Kate from a deep dreamless sleep around nine p.m., and for a moment she froze on the long sectional white couch dazed and a bit confused. As the dim light from the streetlight shined through the half-drawn curtain, she sat silent and listened. Another sound broke through; this one she recognized as the sound of Erin's phone ringing in the kitchen.

Racing to the back room, she yawned before lifting up the receiver. "Hi, this is Kate." No one answered her so she said, "Hello."

A whispered voice said, "Kate."

"Yes, who is this?" She stood up straighter and rearranged the bundled t-shirt back down over her lacy-edged bra. "Could you speak up? I can barely hear you."

"Kate, I need your help."

"Erin?" She stood taller and dragged in a frightened breath. "Is that you?"

"Go to the Hunter home."

The voice sounded frantic; fear registered through the phone line to Kate's trembling body. "I think Matt's Mom is in danger."

"What?"

"Please hurry." The voice sounded softer now. "And please, no police."

"I have to call...."

"No." Frantic again, the whispered tone raised a bit in pitch. "You must not call the police. Go there. Help her."

The other phone landed hard in its cradle and she banged hers down a mere second later. Grabbing the house keys from her purse, she raced out into the chilly night and moved on bare feet to the small flower-lined single-story structure at the left.

She laid her hands on the cool front window and peered into the dim living room. The streetlight behind her showed the room clearly. All looked normal, nothing seemed out of place. Mrs. Hunter's home was as she'd remembered it from her first meeting, the furniture still placed in perfect order with the old-fashioned doilies still hanging just right over the arms of the couch and recliner.

Building anxiety threatened to stop her heart as she stepped from the window to the front door. Leaning her blonde head close to the door, she listened for any sound before encircling her numb fingers around the handle. Surprise sent a rush of fearfulness through her as she stumbled almost fell into the darkened living room. She grabbed the edge of the door and froze, exposed to anyone who may be hiding there.

Nothing moved, no strange sounds sang into her eardrums.

"Mrs. Hunter?"

Nothing.

"Are you here?"

Her question was answered with only empty air.

"Mrs. Hunter?" Kate held her breath, letting it out slowly before stepping into the living room and stopping at the edge of the flower-patterned sofa near the fireplace. She grabbed up the closest thing to use as a weapon—one of the large brass candleholders from the top of the fireplace ledge. Her fingers tightened around the cool object, and she felt strength flow into her body. The weapon-like apparatus gave her a bit more security and she tightened both hands hard around the heavy stick as she walked through the living room toward the hallway leading into the bedroom area.

Stopping at the first door, she stood silent and listened to the quiet around her. No sound could be heard in the room beyond the door so she removed her left hand from the makeshift weapon and placed it on the door handle.

A sharp noise at the front of the house froze her near the half-opened bedroom door and she swallowed her breath. Real fear erupted in her system now. Sleuth-like sounds of a person moving through the living room sent her heart racing in her chest, her breath burning hot in her lungs, and sent her frozen body into a slow slide through the opening.

Soft footsteps sounded closer, loud in the quiet house. She slid her trembling body into the space between the wall and door and closed her eyes tight, clutching the weapon in sweaty hands. She pulled in a quiet breath, forcing her heartbeat to slow to a more manageable level. If she didn't start controlling her heart beat and erratic breathing, this intruder would easily find her. She needed to calm down so she could think through this dangerous situation. Where was Mrs. Hunter? Was she hiding, fearful of the intruder too?

Oh, why had she come running over here on her own? What a stupid thing to do, Kate thought. She should've ignored the whispery voiced command not to call the cops, and let the professionals take care of it.

A creak then a second one sounded close—probably just on the other side of the door. She closed her mouth on empty lungs and a racing heart. Too late to change things now, she thought tucking her body tight to the wall. The door moved slowly toward her, threatening to trap her against the hard surface in a deadening embrace. Side stepping a stealthy inch at a time to the opened closet area half a wall length away, she slid into the darker interior of the small closet and crouched down.

A familiar outdoorsy scent assaulted her first. Mere seconds later a large hand reached in, took hold of her arm, and jerked her out of the crouch. She felt herself being twisted around. And suddenly she was pinned against the footboard of the twin bed.

She screamed, slamming her hands up hard into

a wide chest and striking her bare foot against the side of a pair of loafers. Her assailant only tightened his grip on her forearm. She thrust forward and leaned away from him before raising the candlestick holder with both hands. She pointed it like a knife toward the dim chest area and stabbed hard, grinning at the groan and harsh swear word coming from the man's mouth. With all her might, she heaved the object at him. Then she jerked free of his grip and raced into the living room.

"Damn it." A deep bass voice roared, stopping her near the sofa and loosening the beats of her heart into a rapid rush of a thundering waterfall. She recognized that voice.

"Matt," she whispered. "No!"

He lifted her off her feet and threw her down on the red and green flowered sofa, capturing her hands high up over one of the armrests. She whispered his name again, feeling the heat burning off his body like rays of a tanning bed in the middle of a Seattle rainstorm.

"Matt."

"Kate?" Mint scented breath breezed over her face, sending her heart rate once again dangerously out of control. "Damn it, I could have hurt you."

Jerking up off her melting body, he moved to the nearest lamp and switched it on before twisting around to face her. Nothing showed on his impassive face. "Sit up."

"Matt."

"Get up." Dark eyes glared at her, focusing on the exposed expanse of her tiny middle. "And you might as well cover up, it won't work on me."

"*What* won't work on you?"

"I don't care how sexy you are, how beautiful you look laying there in the dim light, TopNotch Security is not going to finance that damn television show." He glared harder at her. "I don't know what Erin was trying to do, bringing you here, but it won't work. My answer is *still* no."

Chapter Three

"I said, get up."

"Why? What have I done to you?"

He glared at her question. "Just get up."

"What have I done?" Kate jumped from the couch and stepped away from it, circling around the furious man to the front door. "Once again, you're not making sense."

"Don't act innocent with me." Matt stood tall and strong in the small room, seeming to take away all the space surrounding the furniture; to pull all the air from the area. "You *are* an actress, after all."

"I *was* an actress, now I'm an attorney."

"Once one, always one," he quipped. "My dad told me that one a long time ago. And...I've found it to be true."

"Sorry to disappoint, but this time your father's crude little saying is all wrong." She pulled at her t-shirt in a sudden need to cover her middle as she moved toward the door. "I would suggest you go tell him that."

"I wish I could."

She spotted a dark hint of sadness glistening in his eyes. A warm feeling of regret formed in her heart, but quickly dissolved as hard arrogant coldness blocked his weaker emotion from her vision.

"Why are you here in my mother's house?" He moved with menacing slowness toward her. She dragged in a deep breath while backing away until the cold surface of the rough door blocked her escape. "Where's my mom?"

"I don't know."

"You don't know why you're here, or where my mom is?"

As she slid along the wall, his left hand settled near her head and, when she jerked away, his right hand slammed hard against the wall near her ear, effectively stopping her movement and trapping her against the door. Fear edged into her being, weakening her knees to the softness of pudding. When he leaned toward her to stare deep into her eyes another type of emotion assaulted her, one just as frightening because it spoke of things best left alone. She may have brought one of the more interesting female characters to life, but in real life, she was not the least bit similar to Monica.

"Kate?"

The woodsy male scent issuing from this man made her wish things could be different, that she could be a complete, total woman without all the baggage.

Why was she thinking like this? She needed to get her mind back on the immediate problem.

"I got a phone call from…" She pushed her spine hard into the solid wood of the front door. He stood as still as a statue, fingers spread wide on each side of her flushed face, empty stare focusing clear on her. As if to say, if you're lying to me, I'll see it in your emotions, acting or not. "I got a call from…"

"You already said that."

Anger burned into her and she clamped her fingers together between their almost touching bodies and pressed her backside even harder into the wooden doorway. Her hands brushed against his hard abdominal muscles for a brief second, sending a rush of heat into her responsive skin. He groaned out a coffee-scented breath and stepped back an inch. Was he reacting to her touch? Still too close, still too far away, she thought in confusion.

"Damn it, Kate." Darkness deepened the gray of his eyes. "Tell me why you're here. I got a call from my aunt Grace."

"Grace?"

"She thought she saw someone stalking outside the house." The fingers of his left hand spread wide as he leaned his head toward her, stopping with his mouth only inches away from hers. So close she could feel the warmth of his breath breezing over her tingling skin. "She must have seen you."

"Stalking?" The word hit her like a bolt of lightning from a clear sky, burning away all the strange exciting feelings his nearness invoked. "You think I'm a stalker?" Punching her clamped hands into his middle, she heard his startled moan as he expelled his breath. She jerked away from his loosened grip. But before she could move even an inch, he gave out a loud "damn" while trapping her hands in his tight fingers and raising her arms high up over her head. The movement brought his body firmly against her, leaving her breathless in a weird kind of anticipation. She kicked her foot out, catching the edge of his calf. "Let me go."

"Stop fighting me."

"Let me go." Fear mixed with the odd sensation, and she jerked her lower body up and against him. "You're hurting me."

"Damn it, Kate."

Glaring into his gray eyes, she pulled her bottom lip into her mouth and grinded her teeth against it.

"Don't do that."

"Let me go."

"Damn it."

A moan roared past the hard words only a moment before his head swooped down to press a hard quick kiss onto her upturned mouth, smashing her teeth into her bottom lip. Unwilling, yet so very willing, her lips opened under his intense pressure.

He pulled back just as abruptly. "No, this is not going to work, Kate."

All the erupting feelings enveloping her turned

into ashes.

"No, I won't allow you to do this to me," Matt said.

She stood frozen to the door, still feeling the effects of their brief kiss as he jerked her arms down from the wall and backed away.

"I won't allow you to pull a 'Monica' on me. I'm not that gullible anymore."

"Pull a...?" A furious ache filled her, tears of rage threatened to overwhelm her. She hadn't been accused of doing something so underhanded in a long time, in a lifetime. "I don't know what you thought I was trying to do here, but that wasn't even—"

"Are you going to deny you're in my mother's house?"

"How can I deny that? You caught me here."

"And that she's not here?"

"If she was here, don't you think she would've come out by now to tell you to stop acting like such a fool?"

A hard look passed through his dark, dark eyes before he said, "And that you and Erin have plans to do a television series together?"

"How did you know about that?" She fisted her hands near her thighs. "What does that have to do with your mother? Or you?"

"It's none of your business how I know about the series." Stepping closer to her, he glared at her with half-closed lids. "Just answer my question; did the two of you plan to do a series together?"

"It's none of your business either, but, yes, we planned to discuss it while I was in town. Neither of us has decided yes or no."

"And you need money to produce it?"

"Erin said she had a possible backer—TopNotch Security. I think that's the name she gave me. Your mother was the one who suggested the company." Eyes widening, she asked, "What does all this have to do with you? You're only Erin's bodyguard, how much money can you possible have?"

"My net worth is close to ten million dollars."

"Ten million." Aghast, she whispered. "What did you do, rob a couple banks?"

"No, it's more like I inherited a security company."

"You own a ten million dollar company?"

"Around that," he said. "At last check."

"But that police officer at the station, and even your own mother, refers to you as a bodyguard."

"For Erin I was, because my mom thought she was being threatened by an old stalker."

"But he went to jail." Fear tightened Kate's voice, causing her teeth to bite her lower lip. He stared at her movement before swerving away. "Erin told me he went to prison."

He actually smiled before a frown settled around his tight mouth, the hint of desire gone now. "He did go to prison."

"Then why did you have to be her bodyguard?" She sighed around her raised hands before stepping past him toward the flowered couch. She sank into the soft cushion and stared up at the still silent man. "She needed one when she was acting, but certainly not now."

"She didn't?"

"Then why were you her bodyguard?"

That smile formed again, softening the edges of his lips. "It was my mom's idea for me to watch her. Erin didn't even know until she caught me hiding behind the hedge shielding her pool from the road."

"Why didn't she know? It seems if she was in danger, you should have told her you're protecting her."

"That was mom's idea, too." His grin deepened as he remembered the time with fondness. "When your friend caught me spying on her." A gentle laugh flowed from deep in his throat, "After your friend told me in a not-so-polite way that she didn't want me following her around, did I realize what my mother and aunt were up to."

"What was that?"

"Think about it." His frown back as he stared hard at her. "A beautiful unattached female, a good-looking unattached male, you can figure out the rest."

"They set up the two of you?" She couldn't help but smile at the thought, but her smile faded quickly when he turned from her. "Your mom's something, isn't she?"

"Yes." The hard-edged suspicious man had returned, and something inside her hurt at the change. "I won't allow her to fool me like that again."

"She loves you."

"Yes." A darting look glared from his eyes, freezing her breath low in her lungs. "I don't plan on falling for another woman who isn't honest with me."

Confused, she muttered. "That's understandable."

"No matter how sexy and alive she is," he added under his breath. "Answer me, Kate, if you and Erin were still in the discussion stage of doing that movie, why did you authorize your Seattle office to send me the revised script yesterday?"

"You received the revision from the writers? That's strange."

"Strange?"

Hot anger burned in her middle at the sarcasm riding in that one word. "Yes, strange. I haven't even seen the revision. My assistant was supposed to send the script to Erin not you. I didn't have any way to send you anything because Erin never sent me the information I requested about TopNotch."

"Is this true?"

An aching sadness laced through her system, weakening her anger. She just didn't care any more. "You're determined to think the worst of me."

"I'm only searching for the truth."

"The truth?" She lifted up from the couch and took a few steps toward him, stopping before him. "I don't believe you would even know the truth if you heard it."

"Kate?"

"Go find your mother, Matt."

"Matthew, Kate." His tiny mother's sudden appearance in the open front door left her slightly uneasy. How long had she and Grace been standing there? Both women showed signs of despair in their stances, signs of puzzlement in their eyes. "Why are you two fighting? You're not supposed to be fighting."

Kate moaned out her own despair as the situation came to full light.

****

The worst thing that could possibly happen to Matt was happening. He needed to move back from this woman who'd captured his heart so many years ago, and still seemed to have a grip on it now. He'd thought those foolish teenage boy wishes had been subdued by his years of the real thing, but he'd been wrong. It'd only taken one look at the actress' gorgeous face and fit, sexy body to bring the memories roaring hot to the surface of his mind.

And that damn kiss. Why the hell had he kissed her? With every cell in his body, he'd needed to do it. With every part of him, he'd needed to feel her tight body trapped against him.

Because his past, in the form of a rubber-band bundle of letters and a year's worth of journal entries in a box in his old bedroom, connected him to her in a way he'd never admitted to anyone. The knowledge of those letters would give her too much power over him. He couldn't allow it to happen. The past needed to stay dead and buried, along with the memory of the kiss he should never have stolen from her.

"Mrs. Hunter, I got a call from…someone who said you were in danger." Her tone warmed over him like honey over a biscuit right out of the oven, sweet and hot. "I don't understand why someone would do that. I raced right over here to make sure you were all right."

"I'm fine."

"Why would someone call me then?" The tone of her voice deepened to a low alto, sending a rush of burning heat into him. "That's so cruel."

Cruel, he thought. What's cruel is having a voice like that? A voice that was meant to seduce, to confuse a man until he couldn't think straight. Her voice hadn't changed.

"A prank," his mom replied. "I'm fine, dear."

"It was probably that rotten little boy from a few houses down." Grace huffed at her friend. "He needs a whipping, if you ask me. That boy is trouble waiting to happen."

"Whipping little boys is frowned upon around this area, Grace." Looking back at her friend with a wink, Esther added, "If you get caught."

Grace laughed.

"So you actually believe Kate got a phone call, telling her you were in trouble?"

"Why wouldn't we believe her, nephew?"

He stood back on his heels.

"Why else would she come over here without being invited?"

"Fine, Aunt Grace, I get your point."

"You would think it was too clear even to question."

"Remember his sixteenth year, Grace," his mom said, glancing at Kate. "That should explain a lot."

Grace grinned at Esther before turning her wide smile on him. "Oh, yeah, I remember that year."

"What happened?"

Kate's sexy voice warmed through the air and into his heated body, knifing a powerful ache of

39

desire through his groin muscles.

"Those smiles on your faces are very...telling," Kate added.

"Only to some people," his mom said before slicing her glance quickly over his face. "Some people are too busy hiding from the truth to see anything at all."

"I'm not hiding from anything, Mom." Denial sounded easy coming from his mouth, the belief that his denial was right sat hard in his heart. "I see things way too clearly."

Grace leaned into the space separating them. "Boy, you wouldn't see a freight train if it was a foot from you."

"Grace, let it alone."

He watched his honorary aunt nod and grin before stepping past his mother and leading the four of them into the kitchen. He settled into the last red and white chair and watched as Kate fumbled with a saltshaker directly opposite him.

"Don't let Grace upset you, Kate," his mom said.

"She didn't, Mrs. Hunter."

"And, please, call me Esther."

"No, she won't call you Esther." He needed to stop this intimacy from spreading. His mom was way too trusting. "She will not call you Esther."

His aunt asked, "Why not?"

"Aunt Grace, you need to stay out of this."

"Matt." His tiny mother stood straight and formidable, glaring her best motherly look of righteousness into his downward angled face. He moved an inch from her outraged anger. "*You* are the son, I am the mother. I will have anyone I wish call me by my given name."

"But Mom, you don't understand." Kate stared at him through half-closed lids. It was her 'Monica' look of cunning quietness. "She'll hurt you."

"You're a bastard."

He leaped from his chair and stood away from

the table. Hot fire burned deep in her eyes as long fingers clamped around the forgotten crystal-like saltshaker.

"How dare you accuse me of wanting to hurt this kind woman?" Kate pushed away from the table, saltshaker still clutched in her hand. "How dare you?"

"He's my son." His mother's soft voice swept through him, and he jerked his look from the sexy woman's tense figure. "I love him for it. He means well."

"My brothers love my mother, too and they don't act this way."

He watched the little red crop-top lift up and down with each of her breaths, leaving a sight of smooth soft skin exposed. He wanted to touch that narrow strip of skin, to caress it with his thumb. His middle reacted to the exposed skin with every movement; his hands tingled with the memory of her pressed so tight against him.

"But they would never accuse one of their female friends of trying to hurt her," Kate added.

"Like hell." He tore into her. "You think you can use my mother to get your way? Erin tried to use her, too. I won't allow it."

"You won't allow it?"

For a moment, he was positive the saltshaker clamped in her fingers would fly into his face. He even bent down to get away from the worst of it. Yet nothing happened. Instead calmness settled over her, and with it, an aching tiredness.

"I give up." She placed the shaker on the table and walked from the kitchen. The front door closed with a soft click a moment later. If she'd slammed the door, he wouldn't feel so bad now.

"That didn't go well at all."

"No, Esther, it didn't."

"What are you two going on about now?" He jerked around to face the two puzzled women.

"Mom?"

"Oh, son, why are you so determined to ruin everything?"

"Ruin what?"

"I remember a time when that woman made your heart sing."

"Be serious." Warm memories from a past he couldn't quite forget overwhelmed him. The memories of a sad fatherless boy who'd latched onto a dream. "It wasn't my heart that was singing, Mom. I was sixteen and what I felt…about Katherine was pure lust, the same as every other male capable of feeling anything at all."

"You can tell yourself that if you want, Matt." His mom's arm slid around his waist, pulling him close, but he couldn't relax. He refused to be comforted by her embrace. Looking up at him with sad, determine eyes that made him anxious, she said, "But I still have the journal you wrote after your father's death, and the letters. That actress— Katherine touched you more than just in the lower extremities of your body."

Grace laughed. Matt groaned while stepping back from her.

"Deny it all you want, Matt," she said, "But it'll still be true."

"You still have those letters?"

"Yes, and I'm not giving them up."

A cold dread froze him in his tracks. "I want them—now."

"No."

"Mom."

"Those are my insurance policy."

His cold dread changed into heated anger. "I won't allow you to show them to her."

Esther only glanced at Grace and smiled in her sweet cunning way. "If things don't work out the way I want them to, I guess she'll have to read them."

"No, I forbid it."

"Dense, Esther, your boy is completely dense."

****

How could one single man send her emotions in twenty different directions in less than an hour? Kate truly wanted to know the answer to that question. From fear to anger to lust and back to anger were more emotions than she'd experienced in a long time. No man had ever had her so confused, so surprised, so damned turned on in a long while.

She wasn't having any of it.

Unlocking the door of Erin's house, she slammed it shut behind her before throwing the keys in the kitchen. She watched them slide under the stove next to the back door, and groaned.

Great. Now she'd have to get on her hands and knees to retrieve the frigging keys from beneath that large appliance.

"Damn that man." Why he disturbed her so much she would never understand. But why he seemed so quick to think the worst of her she understood completely. He saw her as that character *Monica* and nothing she did or said would ever convince him Monica was only a character in a show. She had lived with this dread for fifteen years, hoping, praying that no one would recognize her as the person who'd played that woman. Lately she'd been lucky. Her older fans had always known her well, yet that man seemed to know her way better than any of the others. The way Matt had acted when they'd first met, something about the way his two elderly relatives acted when he was nearby, some of their strange statements spoke a deep familiarity with her former self.

How old was he anyway? He had to be in his early thirties at least; probably a few years younger than her. That would mean he was at least fourteen or fifteen when "Midnight Revenge" came out in the theaters. The perfect fantasy age. Was he one of those strange men who used to write her suggestive letters and send nasty pictures? Somehow, she doubted it.

No, Matthew Hunter's net income was in the millions. He didn't need to send filthy letters and pornography to get a woman to want him. All he had to do was flash his brilliant smile, flexed his tight muscles and he'd have any woman, of any age, salivating all over him in seconds.

Well, no flashing smile or hard body would get her attention.

No matter how hot that man's quick kiss had been. No matter how tight his muscles, she wasn't falling for his good-looking rich playboy routine. He would no doubt find her a disappointing lover anyway when he realized she wasn't even close to being a 'Monica'. Just like all the other men she'd been out with in the three years since her husband's death. After trying so hard to compete with the character she'd brought to life fifteen years ago, and not succeeding, she had decided to forego the questionable pleasure of dating. Her ego couldn't stand the rejections.

Kate sighed as she moved into the kitchen, grabbed a spatula from the drainer, and dropped on her knees in front of the stove. Luck was with her when the keys slid easily from beneath the white appliance. Placing them onto the counter, she yanked the phone from its cradle and dialed her work number. She groaned, remembering it was after ten at night both here and in Seattle. She would have to wait until morning to find out why her assistant sent Matt a copy of the revisions for the pilot episode of the television series "Three Sisters".

Matt, she thought. A sudden image of how the man looked when he'd trapped her against the wall left her aching, left her wishing she was more like 'Monica' after all.

The phone ringing in her hands tore those images gratefully from her mind, bringing her back to the reality of her lonely life. Her breath caught in her throat, heart racing fast and quick in her chest. Several in and out breaths helped calm down her reaction to the normal sound. It wasn't the sound of the phone that had her heart racing out of control and her breath fighting to fill her lungs. It was the memory of a quick hot kiss, a stolen kiss that should never have happened.

She sat down in one of Erin's sand-colored kitchen chairs. "Hello, this is Kate Williams."

"Kate?" a voice whispered in the phone. "You were at Esther's house?"

"Who are you?" Her temper threatened to overwhelm her at the sound of the prankster's voice. "Mrs. Hunter was fine. How dare you call me and frighten me that way?"

"I didn't call," the voice whispered. Louder was added, "Was she in danger?"

"No, she wasn't." Kate jumped up from the chair and wandered to the window. Quiet darkness filled the expanse of lawn between her and Esther's home. Was Matt still there? Sprouting more lies about her to his mom? "She wasn't hurt, but I could have been."

"How?"

"Her son showed up."

"Matt showed up," the whisper deepened, changed, "I didn't want you to…"

Something was wrong here. "Why did you tell me she was in danger? Who are you anyway?"

Silence lingered on the line except for anxious sounding breaths.

"Are you still there?"

"Things are not as they seem, Kate."

"What?"

"Watch out for yourself." The voice whispered louder, sending another rush of wrongness into her mind. "Things are not as they seem."

"What things?" A dial tone greeted her question

and fear slid into her mind for a brief moment until she shook it away. "Hello?"

What was going on around here anyway?

Chapter Four

The rest of the week went quick for Matt, with only fleeting glimpses of his mother's newest neighbor coming and going from the house next door. On Wednesday morning he decided just to stay away from his mother's altogether. The woman had barely looked his way the two times they'd gotten close enough to speak, barely sang out in that sexy alto voice a simple hello.

He should be happy with her attitude, but he wasn't happy at all.

Because he missed that voice of hers, all warm and sexy, oozing promises and sweetness, and that radiant full smile with those white teeth biting into her bottom lip when she was upset.

Dense, his Aunt Grace had called him. Yes, dense would be a good description of him now. But no way were those two old ladies going to use those old letters to get their wish; no way would he allow them to mess with his past. He'd destroy the proof of his infatuation—along with that damn journal— before he'd allow his mother to show them to that woman.

Dense he may be, but no one would ever call him stupid.

The side alleyway came back into view slowly as he straightened up near the window, the sounds of pounding and male voices echoing in the air. The grimy litter-filled back area of his new headquarters greeted his eyes and he grinned at his own wandering thoughts. For a good ten minutes he'd been staring with unseeing eyes at the empty

47

dumpster near the building, at the thousands of small pieces of garbage blowing around it in the slight breeze of the afternoon wind.

Damn, but that woman had her own type of power. If Carlos could see him now, he would never hear the end of it.

"Enough," he whispered, "Get out of my head, sexy lady."

His whispered words galvanized him to move back to the small, paper-covered desk and sink into the old chair. Grabbing up one of the folders at random, he opened it and forced his mind to study the words. Two hours later all twenty-one of Hotchkiss' former employee's records were separated into two piles, one that threatened to topple over as he placed the last folder on top. He gathered up those fourteen files and placed them on the only other flat surface in the small room—the second chair—and stared at the smaller pile.

A kick on the bottom half of the office door raised his stare and he smiled at his friend's overloaded arms. Matt watched as he set a laptop down on the edge of the desk before throwing the bags of food on the chair, sending the pile of folders to the floor.

Matt moaned.

Carlos placed the unopened laptop toward the middle of the disk and shrugged. "Sorry. I'll pick them up. You better eat before the food gets cold."

"No harm done." He stepped from his chair and moved around the desk to help retrieve the scattered papers that had landed in a bundle next to the still intact file folders. Thankfully only a few individual pages escaped two or three separate files. Fourteen neatly stacked files once again sat together on the floor far from the door a mere minute later, protected by a large wastebasket.

"The hamburgers are cold."

"And the drinks are warm." Matt grinned at his

friend as he pulled a long swallow of iced tea through the straw. "But it's fine. Until you brought the food I didn't even realize it was lunchtime, or that I was hungry."

"I could go out and reorder the meal." Carlos glanced up from his unwrapped burger. "I should have left my laptop in the lobby, but—"

"I don't think any of the construction workers would mess with it." Matt bit into his still-warm burger and swallowed the huge bit. "You didn't take it with you when you went to get lunch, did you?"

"I didn't have to go get lunch today." Carlos sipped his iced tea while glancing at the flat object in front of him. "Believe it or not, one of the office ladies we inherited from Hotchkiss asked me if I wanted something to eat when she went out to order for the rest of the staff."

"Good," Matt said, "I'm glad the older employees are warming up to us."

"It was inevitable," Carlos said with a smirk. "We're too friendly and handsome to be ignored for long. And some of those ladies are mighty fine."

"I won't tell Mary," he grinned, "that you're checking them out."

"Keep it up, Hunter." The insult didn't faze the man.

"None of the ladies here even come close to my Mary."

Matt laughed.

Carlos grinned. "You're just pissed that the computer nerd got a good woman to marry him before the dumb blond jock."

Shining sky-blue eyes stealing into his mind slammed him back in his chair. He pushed the image down to a safer place. His friend already sensed too much about his interest in the woman. "Yeah, Mary's a joy."

"But then how many dumb blond jock-types really want to settle down and get married? It'll cramp your style."

His style, Matt thought.

"But then again you've been without for what, six months now?" Throwing his sandwich wrapper into the bag, he stared at him with intense dark eyes. "Maybe your style has changed since...Anna."

"Maybe."

His intensity forced Matt to crinkle his empty hamburger wrapper.

"Yeah, and maybe it's time you got back into the game."

He didn't comment, only continued to stare at the colorful paper crumbled up in his hand and the half-filled red fry box.

"Just tell me to back off, man."

"Back off, Carlos."

His friend's mouth gaped opened for a moment at the slight violence in his words. Silence filled the air around the two as they finished their lunch, only broken occasionally by the sounds of hammering and pounding. When Carlos gathered up all the wrappers and placed them in the trashcan next to the folders, he reached and moved his laptop to the center of the desk.

Matt indicated the smaller pile of folders to his left. "I should've never promised Mr. Hotchkiss I would keep all his employees after buying the company."

"Why?" Carlos pulled the folders to him and looked at the top name. Typing it into the employee's database, he skimmed over it quickly. "How old is this guy anyway? Seventy? Oh, I see, he's sixty-seven."

"There are at least three others that age, or close to it."

Carlos glanced up from the screen. "So what's wrong with this guy? You know the law. Age isn't an issue you can use to fire someone."

"It should be in his case and the two others,

who're older." He sighed and leaned back in his chair. It groaned under his two hundred pounds in a less than peaceful way. "But it's their health I'm really worried about. All three smoke and are a good thirty pounds overweight. They couldn't have been to see a doctor in years."

"You can't discriminate because of weight either."

Matt picked up the top folder and slammed it back down on the desk in front of him. "I wish I could."

Carlos nodded in agreement. "And the other four?"

"At least they're healthy," answered Matt. "But they're another type of problem completely. Why he kept those four lazy...men on is beyond me. He's a better man than I'll ever be."

"Are they really that bad?"

"Check it for yourself."

While Carlos perused the other four names, Matt dragged out his own laptop and opened up his email. Load groans and soft sighs sounded across the room as the smaller man read through the personnel files. Matt ignored him as he read through one last email. "I don't believe this."

"What's wrong?"

Matt turned his screen so Carlos could read the e-mail he'd just received. "It's from one of the producers of that damn series, 'Three Sisters'. Why in the hell is he e-mailing me? I haven't changed my mind about backing the series."

The printer started spilling out sheets as Carlos gazed at Matt's screen. "He's setting up an appointment to meet with you. I'm confused."

Three double-spaced sheets leaped into the printer's tray. Matt stared at the pages for a moment before retrieving the computer and rereading the message.

Mr. Hunter,

As you're well aware, I'm involved with the production of a possible new television series tentatively called 'Three Sisters'. You should have received the pilot script from the head writer already. I'm interested in meeting with you some time next week. I realize you're in the middle of reorganizing your company so I'll leave the time—and the place— up to you.

I'm looking forward to finally meeting you, sir.

Howard Brown

"Who in the hell is this Howard Brown guy anyway?" Matt slammed his hand on the desk before leaping from the chair. "I've never heard of him."

"I've no clue, man." Carlos stood to retrieve the pages from the printer. "That's a mystery to me. We may not have a clue about him, but at least we have some ammunition to use against those seven Hotchkiss employees we might need to get rid of."

"I hope so."

"We'll have fire to use against the seven if we decided to let them go." Carlos glanced up from the pages. "And you're right about not being as good as Hotchkiss."

Matt closed up the lid of his laptop, deciding to leave the manner of Howard Brown alone. The moving of TopNotch's headquarters to Brookville was his top priority at the moment; the mystery of who Brown was could wait until tomorrow.

"According to their files," Carlos continued, "Mr. Hotchkiss put up with a lot of shit from those four men."

"I've noticed that." Matt took the pages from his partner while glancing out the small window. The sun shined bright into his eyes, and he watched it slowly settle to the west. "I really want to do right by the man."

"Yeah." Carlos sank back into his chair and stared at his screen again. "The best we can hope for is if these men are willing to give us a chance." He shook his head, the glaring overhead light hit against his centered bald spot. "I think things will turn out all right."

"A security firm in my hometown would be the one giving me the hardest time," Matt said. "I should've never decided to move TopNotch's headquarters here."

"And your mother would've wondered why you didn't want to live near her." He grinned. "And that crazy aunt of yours would've never let you hear the end of it."

"But I would've never met Anna."

"Or Kate," whispered Carlos. "How many people ever get the chance to meet their all-time fantasy woman?"

He glanced down at his closed laptop before leaping out of his chair. The view from the window hadn't changed. "Yeah, some fantasy."

If only it was that simple, Matt thought. Why couldn't she have gotten fat and gray, wrinkled and old? Why did she still have to look so good?

And why did he suddenly receive a script and an e-mail from one of the series producers a few days after her arrival in California?

"Are you doing anything on Saturday night?"

"What?" Taken aback, Matt jerked to face his friend. "Why are you asking me that?"

Carlos grinned. "Mary has someone she wants you to—"

"No."

"Man, be reasonable."

"No." He softened his answer. "I know Mary means well but I'm not ready to date again."

Carlos only stared at him. "Okay, I'll accept that."

"Tell Mary we'll do it some other time."

The intensity in Carlos' eyes alarmed him, causing Matt to glance quickly out the window again. The litter-filled alleyway disappeared as a tall, womanly figure with laughing sky-blue eyes and soft blonde hair filled his mind, and a memory of a sexy, throaty voice rang in his ears.

"Yeah, next time," Carlos said.

His friend surrendered, but something in his demeanor spoke volumes to Matt.

"But I hope you say yes next time."

"Carlos?"

"Mary won't take no as an answer twice in a row."

Neither did a certain ex-actress turned lawyer, Matt thought.

****

Kate almost missed the entrance to the playhouse center for a second time as she slowed the rental car and backed up onto the tree-lined winding road. The afternoon sun shone in her eyes as she turned into the hidden entrance and drove up to the large building. Normally she would have just driven around the block again and hoped she saw the opening on her next pass by, but twice was enough. She stopped and pulled into the shadowy parking lot and breathed in astonishment when she spied the modern building: narrow and long with glass enclosing the whole front wall. To the right of the structure stood an older, yet fashionable dark wooden playhouse, oval in shape and well maintained with strategically placed trees and brushes to soften its edges. Joyful voices could be heard yelling and laughing inside the oval structure; a group of people could be seen standing at the wide front entranceway.

Peace broke through her unease and for the first time since arriving in Brookville and finding Erin gone, she felt good about her situation. Erin had smoothed over Kate's troubled feelings with her quick e-mail, but she still didn't feel quite right about being here.

Shaking off her uneasiness, she slid out of the

car and turned toward the building. A familiar young male voice called out her name, stopping her with her hand on the smooth cool doorknob of the glass door.

"We're over here."

She glanced over toward the oval building. "Billy, where are you?"

"Over here, by the entrance."

"Oh, I see you now." She dropped her hand and stepped toward the older building. "I'm sorry I'm so late but I overslept. I had a hard time getting to sleep last night. I hope it's not a problem."

"Oh, it's okay." Billy stared at her, flushing as his eyes spotted the light tan skin exposed by her chop-top and low-riding jeans. "You look nice today."

She smiled at his wide-eyed reaction, feeling safe, beautiful and sexy, all at the same time. "Why, thank you."

She watched him shake his head hard before he finally moved his look from her middle to the ground. Moving toward the boy, she touched the top of his buzzed-cut hair. "You're not looking too bad yourself."

His flushed face lifted up to peer at her, reddening even more as the warmth of her smile moved over him. "Well, we should get inside. I mean, everyone is waiting for us. For you."

"Lead the way." Inside, a mix of people sat around the hodge-podge of chairs and tables in front of a raised stage area. An orchestra practiced a familiar set of chords before starting a pretty song she'd never heard before; a beautiful soprano voice sang the words to the sweet ballad. "Oh, what a beautiful voice."

"We were supposed to do the show 'Our Town', but the director changed her mind." Billy seemed a bit disappointed. "I preferred to keep to our first choice."

"Why is that?"

He blushed before saying, "I can't sing."

She smiled over at him. "To tell you the truth, I'm not that good either."

"But Sally, now...my sister can really sing. She's great!" Pride sounded clear in his voice. "She's great. Just wait and I bet you'll agree with me. That's her singing now, a song from the musical 'The Sound of Music'."

"That's Sally?" Impressed, she turned toward the sweet voice. "Wow."

"She's the talent in the family."

The boy shrugged, a deep look of envy mixed with pride fought in the tanned features of his face, pride won.

"I'm not all that talented."

"Now, why do I find that hard to believe?" Kate punched him lightly on his arm, and smiled. "Have they started casting this show yet?"

"No, we were waiting for Ms. Fitzgerald to get here. Or rather you."

"Well, I'm here." Kate grinned wide. "Let's get this show on the road, as they say in the business."

"Yeah, right." Shaking his dyed blond and black head, he pointed toward the racket of loud speaking and singing voices that mixed in a frightful way with the contrasting sound of the well-directed band music. "Come on, Mrs. Williams."

"So what play are you doing, anyway? The Sound of Music?"

"You recognize that song?" He hummed a bit of the slightly familiar tune along with her. And he was right about not being able to sing, he could barely hum in tune.

"It's a good thing they have some speaking parts."

"It's a good thing you're the advisor." He mimicked her. "That way you'll still have a job when the casting is done."

"You're a funny one, kid."

"Billy?" His sister stood with hands on hips, staring daggers at the grinning boy. "Where have you been? We've been waiting here forever."

"Me and Mrs. Williams have been having a conversation."

"You should have let her come in when she first arrived." Her pout spoiled the beautiful lines of her round face. "You know we've been waiting almost an hour."

"Why don't you just chill for a bit, little sister?"

A deep male voice broke up the small fight. "Billy. Sally."

"Dad, Billy kept Mrs. Williams outside."

Sally's whining tone scratched against the edge of Kate's spine, rattling down the curve of it.

"You told him to bring her in as soon as she arrived," the girl added.

"I said that's enough, Sally."

"But Dad."

"I'll take care of your brother later." Kate watched the man glance in her direction while sighing loud under his breath. "If you want to be a part of this production, you'd better get out there and sign up."

"Dad?"

"Sally, I'm not arguing with you about this."

A pout formed around her tight mouth, and she suddenly envied this man's seeming ease as the stout girl turned and ran behind her laughing brother onto the stage.

"Teenagers," he said.

"I hear they can be a handful."

"It was so much easier when they were young." The man watched his two children get into a line forming around a long rectangular table in front of the stage. He shook his head as he turned to smile at her. "I guess I should introduce myself—I'm Joseph Hawthorn. I'm in charge of just about everything involved with the designing and putting together of one of these amateur musical."

"You mean the sets and costumes? That must be a time consuming job for you."

"It sure is but I get a lot of help from the non-acting members of this committee. And my son. He's a whiz when it comes to designing a stage set area." The uplifting of lips reached clear to his sparkling eyes. "We are the first ones here and the last ones to leave."

"They seem like good kids."

"I should apologize for that boy of mine though, and Sally too." The harsh words turned softer as he stared toward the two bickering teenagers. "Those two can fight about everything, or nothing. I'll talk to them about it tonight. It won't happen again."

"It didn't bother me, Mr. Hawthorn."

"Call me Joe, and I'll drop it."

"It's a deal, Joe."

Taking her outstretched hand, he squeezed it quickly before dropping it and moving toward the elongated table. "I'll introduce you to the director, Emily Walsh. You'll be working closely with her. You'll like her."

"I'm sure I will."

"Oh, one other thing," he said, stopping next to the table, "It's nice to meet the fifth most wanted actress of the last decade."

"I was hoping you wouldn't recognize me."

"Why? Erin didn't seem to mind when anyone recognized her."

"Erin's different from me." Kate had always found it so hard to explain to a non-acting individual why she wanted her past to stay in her past. "My name's Kate now, and I would love if you called me that."

"Kate it is."

His confused look told her he didn't understand her reasoning behind her insistence. "I'll call you anything you wish, but that's not going to stop people from recognizing you."

"I'm just Kate."

The man nodded in her direction, and relief flowed through her system when he dropped the whole thing and walked away. She didn't think about it at all for the next fifteen minutes as one person after another stopped to talk with her. Some showed signs of recognition; some didn't, but all accepted her as Kate Williams. She would never be able to remember all the names and all the different faces, but some of the voices she'd never be able to forget. Especially Sally's sweet, rich soprano as it rang out in the quiet air of the playhouse. An untrained voice, yet one that made your heart hurt with the beauty of it.

"It's a pity we haven't got a bigger part for a girl her age to play." A sharp faced young woman sat down next to her. "The closest part we have for her is the second to oldest daughter. Anna is going to have some stiff competition for the lead roles in a few years, and I can't wait."

"Anna?"

"You're Erin's friend, right?" Without waiting for an answer, the take-charge woman grabbed her hand and squeezed it tight. "It's Kate, right? Billy told me you'd be taking over Erin's advising duties until she returns to California."

"Yes, she'll be back by next week. I think."

"Joe. Max. Let's get this started. We're twenty minutes behind schedule." The young woman slammed the clipboard she'd held like a weapon in her hands hard atop the table. "I think we've all meet our new advisor, Kate, so I think its time we start the auditions."

"I take it you're the director, Emily."

"Oh, I'm sorry." Smiling for the first time, the young woman reached out and grabbed her hand into another tight, quick grip. "It's nice to meet one of Erin's friends. If you're as good at this as Erin is, you'll be a major asset for us."

"Thank you."

Turning back to the raised stage, the friendliness in the woman's face and voice were gone. "We'll start with the reading parts."

****

The try-outs went well when Emily got the group in some semblance of order and the people began reading for different parts. And Billy was right about his sister. She was amazing, both with the acting and the singing. Billy was also right about one other thing; the poor boy had no acting or singing ability at all. Within two hours everyone who wanted to try-out for a part had a chance to audition, and a nervous edginess lingered in the air around her. Kate remembered the nervousness well. After every one of her auditions, she'd felt this restless jumpy feeling carousing through her body.

"I'm going to consult with Kate and get back to you on my final choices by next Wednesday." Emily looked around the quieting room. "You've all done a fine job. It's going to be hard to make the right selections, but by our next practice I'll have the list of parts posted at the door."

Kate smiled at the woman's obvious lie. Some of the people sitting with such hopeful expression brightening in their eyes would be disappointed come Wednesday. Most of the actors would be more valuable to Joe, doing off-stage work.

"It's not fair." She muttered under her breath. "Billy should be better."

"Did you say something?"

"No, not really, I'm just puzzled by something," said Kate. Pointing to Billy, she said, "He seems like a natural actor, yet..."

Emily laughed. "God works in strange ways sometimes. Billy's great in a small group, but when it comes to large crowds he just freezes up."

"You'd think that Sally would do the freezing."

Kate shook her head, glancing over at the quiet girl sitting all alone up on the stage. "She's so quiet."

"But up on stage, that girl is a dynamo."

Kate grinned at her quick stare. "I've noticed that. In a few years, she'll be getting all the lead parts. She's great."

"I can't wait until that happens." Emily frowned toward the back of the theater and Kate swallowed a breath. "Hey, there's Matt. I didn't think he'd show up for the try-outs."

"Matt?"

"Have you met him yet?" When she started to wave him to them, Kate pulled the director's arm down with a sharp no.

"Oh, I guess you've meet him. I hope he didn't do the same thing to you he did to poor Anna. Have you heard about that?"

"Anna?"

"She's the one that's been getting all the lead female roles for the last four or five years." Emily dragged her hands from her arm and stared at her so intently she wanted to hide. "She's back there with Matt now, still trying to get back together with him. He broke it off with her a good six months ago, but hope springs eternal for all of us."

"Anna and Matt were a couple?" Kate's heart sank in her chest, breath burned hot deep in her lungs. Her reaction surprised her. She didn't even like the man that much. "I didn't know he'd been...I got the impression from Esther and Grace that he'd been so involved with his security business that he didn't have time for well, for anything else."

"For a man like Matthew Hunter, there's always time for women." The young director laughed out so loud and sudden, all the people still sitting jerked in their direction. "Even though he hasn't been with anyone since he broke it off with Anna."

Sally nodded slightly toward Kate, grinning behind the two of them before jumping up quickly and racing toward the silent man standing in the back of the playhouse. Billy grinned in his direction too, but didn't stand from his attention gathering position. As Kate looked around, trying desperately to ignore the man and woman standing so close together at the door, she noticed the usual looks her way from the people following each other out the wide front entrance. But their stares didn't upset her as much as Matt's blank look, as much as Anna's cunning expression. He handed Sally a large manila envelope before touching her cheek lightly and turning to leave the building, with the actress not too far behind.

A coldness settled in Kate's spine at his final look—one of deep disappointment mixed with bright, fiery anger. He barely knew her, so why the anger? What did she do to deserve that hurting look?

The fierce glare burning out of Anna's eyes and hard into Kate's skin like a fresh-sharpened knife. "So I suppose you're going to give the lead to Anna?"

"She's a wonderful singer and actress. She is a bit hard to work with, but she'll give her best when it's time for her to perform." Emily sighed. "In a way, I'm not surprised Matt broke off their engagement."

"They were engaged?" Why this surprised her she wasn't sure. "I wouldn't think a man like that would let any woman trap him into marriage."

"We were all surprised by it." The director grinned at her, pulling at her arm to bring her closer. She lowered her voice, "I always thought he had a thing for Erin, and that's why he broke it off with Anna so fast."

"No, I doubt that."

"Then it must have been someone I haven't met yet." Emily laughed into her startled face, poking her sharp nail into her lower arm. "Hey, maybe it's you. You are Katherine Adams, aren't you? Every man I've known has had the hots for either you or Erin Fitzgerald. Matt's the right age."

"Katherine Adams is gone, I'm Kate Williams now." Turning a pleading look into her direction, she added, "I don't like being referred to as Katherine Adams."

Emily nodded. "The past means nothing to me either." She touched the tip of a finger to her temple. "It's what's here now that counts the most. You're a different person now. Esther told me you're a lawyer from Seattle, that's something to be proud of."

"I don't regret going back to school to finish my English degree, or going on to law school. My husband was so proud of me." Sadness filled her at the memory of the day she'd graduated, how proud and happy Bruce had seemed to be. He was a good man in many ways, ways she'd forgotten in her rush to find her way back to her past. "I've always been a better actress than a lawyer, but my Bruce never gave up on me. He even made me a partner in his firm."

"Mrs. Williams?" Her temporary ache left as she stared down at the stout girl. "Matt asked me to give this envelope to you. I asked him to stay but he said he had to get back to work."

At her blank look, Emily said, "TopNotch Security is moving their headquarters to Brookville."

"Yeah, his company owns a lot of smaller firms all over the Pacific Northwest area." Sally said. "He told my dad he wanted to move into the Midwest or East soon."

"He um, seems like a good man." Dream memories came rushing into her, a conflicting set of images filled with naked touches and unfulfilled desires, fear and slight unease. Every day for the past week she'd awaken frustrated and troubled by the sensual dreams. Vague, sexy, each one more intense than the one before, left her aching in a familiar way. "I can understand why you're so proud of him."

"Yeah, I am." Sally handed her the envelope

before running to the front and jumping up onto the stage. "I'll see you on Wednesday, Emily."

"Sure, and don't be late." Emily stared at the stage for so long Kate started to gather up her things and place them into a neat pile on the table near her. "Can I give you some advice?"

Kate turned to look at the director.

"I would be careful around Matthew Hunter if I were you."

If her dreams didn't stop soon, it might be too late.

"He's on the rebound now, from Anna."

"I'm always careful." Her heart sank in her chest. "I'll be all right."

"Are you sure? Because according to Anna, Matt still loves her and I think she might be right. He's been acting so out of character lately."

"I appreciate your concern, but I'll be all right. Matt and I barely know each other. I'm just his mother's temporary neighbor."

"He's not the way he used to be when he was younger, but he still can hurt you." The woman stared hard at her, trying to read her mind through her closed face. Kate wouldn't allow that. "I have to admit he has settled down in the last two or three years. I believe Anna was probably the last woman he dated seriously until…"

Emily gazed at her, searching for something beyond the blankness. But Kate could still act, could still hide her uneasiness under a blank look of friendly interest. "He really started to settle down when his mom convinced him to be your friend's bodyguard."

"A shameless way to get the two of them together," she said. "Why did she do that?"

The woman laughed. "So you're not fooled by those two conniving little ladies?"

Had he loved Anna so much that his mom needed to take such desperate measures to help him get over her? From the door, the beautiful browned-hair woman stared back at her, a burning look that spoke of unnecessary hatred. "She doesn't seem like Matt's type. She seems too hard."

"I think all the rumors going on about the two of them came from Anna." Emily glance shifted to her clenched hands, and Kate watched her wring her fingers as she tried to find the right words. "What I mean is, yes, they did have a relationship; and yes, they did break it off about six months ago; and yes, Matt hasn't dated since their breakup but, I don't believe his lack of female company has anything to do with that break up."

Kate shouldn't be so interested in the man's past yet she was hanging onto every one of the director's words. Damn, but she was confused.

Why had she ever come to California in the first place? Why was she tempted to do that television show with Erin? And why did she let a man she'd just met and barely knew make her feel so mystified?

"Kate?"

"I'm sorry, my mind was wandering."

"To Matt?" A look of intensity mixed with anxiety in her eyes. "I thought he wanted Erin, but now I'm not so sure."

"No, he didn't want my friend." Fierceness darkened in her voice. "He's not Erin's type."

"Well, it's a mystery I don't understand." Emily reached over to the table in front of them both. "I guess Anna must be right after all; he is still in love with her."

"Why do you say that?"

"If he isn't in love with Erin, he has to still love Anna."

"I don't understand."

"Look, Kate." Throwing all the papers into an old brief case, she slammed it hard before turning to face her. "I've known Matt since his father died and

65

I've never seen him without a woman hanging all over him." She frowned at her. "He's been woman-free for the last six months. There has to be a reason. If he's not in love with Erin than Anna must be telling us the truth, and he must still be in love with her."

Chapter Five

His hand moved over her bare leg, caressing his fingertips over the back of her knees with demanding strokes. Warm breath moved over the damp hair at her nape, sending a rush of heat throughout her system. When his lips touched her bare back, trailing a line of wetness down to the edge of her bathing suit, Kate sighed in her half-sleep.

She wanted to touch him.

The rough fingers stilled at her knees before moving tiny circles over the back of her thighs until his touch reached the curve of her bottom. He spread his fingers wide on her, stretching out his hand to cover her backside with passionate heat while his lips moved up her spine to bite at her exposed ear.

"Ah, Matt."

Hot aching desire flowed through her when his index finger touched the aching area between her legs.

"Matt."

Sweat dropped down the side of her face now, replacing the bite of his gentle teeth on her earlobe. As she opened her eyes to the bright sun overhead, she sighed in frustration.

A daydream. Lying on the lounger in view of her elderly next-door neighbor, she was having a daydream about that same woman's son. It was bad enough waking up frustrated every morning, but now—

"No."

Turning onto her back, Kate raised both knees

up and took in one deep breath after another to erase both the sensual feeling weakening her middle and the protective anger.

She didn't want to move off of the lounger, out of the warm relaxing sunlight. She didn't want to move out of the sexy daydream into the cold reality of her life.

It was bad enough to dream about the man every night.

But now every day she would probably add a daydream or two, daydreams of a man who didn't want to have anything to do with her. If he'd been at all interested, he would've made an attempt to see her. But over a week had passed, and he hadn't said one word.

Pathetic. She was pathetic.

Grabbing her white cover-up from the foot of her lounger, she leaped up and raced into the linen-scented coolness of the house. A cold glass of water chilled her hand a mere second later, and she drank it down in one long gulp while standing at the kitchen sink.

The phone rang as she set the glass into the drainer. "This is Kate."

"Dear, this is Esther."

"Mrs. Hunter?" At the silence on the other end, she said, "I mean, Esther."

"I was wondering if you would like to go with me into town today for lunch."

"I was just...sunbathing."

"That's all right." Without giving her time to say either yes or no, she added, "Grace and I will come get you in about twenty minutes. Will that be enough time for you to get a shower and change into something cool?"

"I don't feel like going into town today."

"I'll allow you thirty minutes, but no more." Before Kate could speak again, the older woman said good-bye and hung up the phone.

"Esther?" The last thing she wanted to do was to meet with Esther and Grace for lunch. "I just had a hot daydream about your son. Do you want to hear about it?"

She grinned at her silliness, wondering what the woman would say if she told her about her nightly dreams. Would she be surprised that the cold-hearted Kate Williams could actually have such sexy dreams at all?

And would she still take her to lunch if she did know the extent of her obsession with her son?

****

"You promised Mary you would say yes," Carlos insisted. "You have to go out with this woman, man."

"She's already got a second date lined up for me?" Matt looked up from the annual financial statement. "It's only been a few days. Tell me something, where is that beautiful wife of yours finding all these potential dates anyway?"

"Oh, they're everywhere you look." Carlos' grin deepened as a pretty dark-haired woman stepped into the small office with a fresh brewed pot of coffee. "They are everywhere you look in this town."

Matt stared at the woman as she poured him a cup. She was one of the assistant's Matt had kept on his payroll while the rebuilding was being finished. Was this the woman Mary wanted him to go out to lunch with?

"Well, what do you say?" Carlos asked.

He watched the woman walk out of the door, her hips swaying with aggressive movements. Nice, he thought. She turned to him and smiled in an easy way before stepping out of his view. She wasn't his first choice of a date, but she would do. His first choice wouldn't even look at him when he went to visit his mother every day. And six months *was* a long time for him to go without a woman warming his bed.

"Maybe I will," said Matt, thinking that she

could be a pleasant distraction from his problems with this change over. "Yeah, why not?"

Carlos frowned. "Good."

"But I don't remember her name." Pointing toward the door, he said, "Carly? Carol? What is it?"

"Oh." Guilt quickened Carlos' voice. "It's Carol."

"I knew it was something like that." Matt stared at his guilty look while standing up to move toward him. He grabbed rough at his shoulder, tightening his grip on the narrow surface. "Don't feel so bad, Carlos, Mary won't find out you told me. I will act surprised when I get to the restaurant."

"Oh, you'll be surprised all right," Carlos murmured.

****

Kate liked the main street of this little town. It reminded her in a way of her old hometown in the middle of Illinois. This California town looked a lot like a Midwestern town, pickups being the vehicles of choice for the majority of the residents. Her small upscale rental car seemed slightly out of place in the small town atmosphere.

And it was super busy now. The café was buzzing with activity, filled with an assortment of people of all ages and races. When Esther and Grace led her to one of the few empty tables near a long window, a pretty waitress walked up to them with two colorful cups and one plain white one, and filled them all with fresh coffee.

"Esther, Grace? What can I get you this afternoon?" She picked a pad of paper out of her pocket and set her pencil tip to the blank page. "The specials are on the board over there."

Kate twisted her head to read the list.

"We'll just take the coffee for now." Esther glanced at her briefly before saying, "I'm expecting a few other people."

"Oh, will that good looking son of yours be joining you?" The waitress patted her short hair into place. "It'll be nice to see him again."

"Esther?" Kate stared at the older woman. "You didn't tell me your son was meeting us."

Guilt lined her face. "I didn't think you would come if I told you."

"Why would you think that?"

"Well, girl, it's been a week and you haven't said as much as one word to the poor boy," Grace answered for her friend. "Did you think we were going to sit back and let that happen for long?"

"Grace?"

"Well, she's not being very friendly toward your son, Esther."

"He hasn't been exactly talkative to me either, Grace." Kate glanced from one wrinkled face to the other, settling on the smaller one. "But you should've told me."

"If you want to leave..." The older woman pointed to the entranceway. "You can leave. We're not holding you here against your will."

"We should though."

"If she doesn't want to have anything to do with my son..." Looking over at Kate, she continued, "We *can't make* her stay."

"That's not it, Esther." Shame sounded in her voice, deepening it a degree lower as Kate looked down at her folded hands on top of the table. "I just don't believe he wants to have anything to do with me."

"Why do you think that?" Esther asked.

"I've been here all week, and he hasn't spoken to me once since our last confrontation." Kate glanced at the menu again. "I guess he's still angry at me over that script. I did see him at the auditions last Wednesday, but he didn't stop to talk. He seemed upset."

"It's not because of you, girl." Grace leaned toward her, placing a large hand on top of her clamped fist. "It's because of that...Anna."

71

"Anna?" Matt's ex-fiancée, she thought. She met her on Wednesday, a fair actress who acted unkind and hateful to all those around her. "She tried out for the musical the people are putting on there. And I think Emily is going to give her the lead role."

"She is a fine actress."

"Yes, but—" Kate choice her next words carefully. "I've known a few actresses much like her. They weren't the easiest people to work with."

"She's a hard one." Grace slammed her fist against the table. "I can't wait until little Sally gets a few years older and starts taking all those lead roles from her. Have you heard that girl sing? She's an angel."

Kate smiled. "Yes, she is. She's going to give Anna some competition in a few years."

"I can't wait," Grace said with feeling. "Anna will finally get what she deserves."

The bell above the entrance door rang, causing the three of them to turn toward it. A lean Hispanic man and a tiny woman walked into the cooled air of the restaurant and waved in their direction. The couple smiled as one when they approached the table.

"Hello, ladies." The man's intense gaze fell onto Kate's face. This man recognized her. "Oh, yeah, you're Katherine Adams. Oh, my name is Carlos Lopez and this is my wife Mary. I work with Matt Hunter."

"Where is my son?"

His glance leaped to Esther.

"She knows about our little matchmaking lunch," Grace said, nodding toward Kate as if she didn't exist.

"Good." Carlos pulled out the chair next to Grace for his wife before sinking down into the one between Mary and Esther, leaving the only empty chair near Kate's left side. That's just wonderful, she thought. "But I'm afraid Matt thinks he's supposed to meet with one of our newer employees."

"Good." His mother leaned into the table. "I like it when my son is unaware of things. He'll act like he's not surprised though."

The waitress returned with two more plain white cups and filled them with coffee before the front doorway opened again and the blond, tanned man wandered into the building. He spied his mother and waved before his wide eyes fell on Kate's upturned face. Freezing in mid-step as if contemplating turning and racing out of the café, Matt finally continued walking toward the table. He didn't look at Kate as he sat in the only empty chair; didn't say hello or acknowledge her in any way. She tightened her fingers into a fist in her lap.

"Mom. Aunt Grace."

"You're being rude, boy."

At his aunt's crude words, he looked over to Kate and nodded a sharp greeting.

"It's good to see you again, Mrs. Hunter." Mary's calming voice brought Kate's look away from the man's angry features. "And you, Aunt Grace."

"Mary, I've told you a million times to call me Esther." The woman's smile encompassed all of them in its brilliant light. "You've always called Grace, Aunt Grace, so why have you never called me Esther?"

"Well, you are my husband's boss's mother."

"So what?" Esther said with a smile. "And from what I understand of their relationship, they're more friends than employer-employee. The two are partners. I want you to call me Esther." Glancing at Kate, she added, "And I wish you would call me that too."

"Mom?"

"Yes, I would *love* to call you by your first name." Fierce temper sliced out of control in Kate's sharp words. "I will call you anything you wish."

Dark eyes glared into her, burning her with

their intense anger. Suddenly a packet of papers in a business sized manila envelope leaped into her mind. Kate had never looked into the envelope. She'd thrown it on the coffee table and as far as she knew it still sat in the exact same place.

Is that why this man seemed so mad at her right now? Whatever was in that envelope must be something discriminating, but what could it possibly be?

"It's going to be the highlight of the season for this small town," Grace was saying as Kate brought her thoughts back to the little group. "Peter loved going to the Chamber of Commerce dinner every year."

"The Chamber of Commerce dinner is always the best." Esther looked at Kate. "I remember going with my husband. It was the biggest party we'd go to every season. My Matthew was always one of the sharpest looking guys there."

"Yes, Matthew was a fine looking man." Grace smiled. "Almost as fine as my Peter."

"What's this about a Chamber of Commerce dinner?" Carlos' slight accent broke into the two women's conversation. "I haven't heard anything about a dinner."

"Matt didn't tell you about it?" Esther looked at her son. "I'm surprised you didn't mention it to him. I hope that you plan on going. TopNotch Security needs to be represented by one of the leaders of the company. Every year since Grace's Peter started the company he's attended the Commerce dinner."

"I haven't even thought of it."

Matt tightened up next to Kate when she reached for her coffee cup, fearful she might touch him. She sighed at his reaction.

"I don't know if I'll be able to attend this year. Carlos and Mary could go in my place."

"No, Carlos and Mary can not go in your place." Grace grabbed at his arm. The man leaned away from his aunt, pushing softly into Kate's side. He pulled away quickly but not until a hint of heat escaped the confines of his suit pants to warm her covered leg. "You'll be going to this one, boy."

"Aunt Grace?"

"You *will* be going."

"Grace, let it go for now." Esther stopped her angry friend with a calming hand on her arm. "I know he'll make the right decision."

Kate had never seen his mother so angry before, and a hint of disquietude lingered in her system for the man.

"We should order lunch before it gets too late," Mary said.

"His Uncle Peter would be so disappointed," accused Grace, "if Matt decided not to go this year."

"Have you decided what you would like to eat?" The same waitress as before stood so near to Matt her arm almost leaned on him. "Honey, I've got you're favorite."

"I'm not hungry." He looked at the woman, not moving away from her intentional touches. "I'll just have coffee."

Kate jerked her glare from the woman's flirty attitude to her coffee cup. Why should it bother her if Matt liked this young woman rubbing against him? It wasn't any of her concern.

"Why don't you just order something, man?" Carlos spoke in the silence. "You haven't eaten anything since breakfast early this morning."

"I could whip up your regular meatloaf and mashed potatoes if you'd like me too."

I just bet you could, Kate thought. What is wrong with her anyway? Glancing up at the pretty waitress who didn't seem to be in any rush to ask the other five people at the table what they'd like to eat. Kate swallowed a hard dry breath before looking back down at her hands. A hot feeling flowed through her body at the wide-eyed cunning look shining from the waitress' eyes, at the way her smile lifted up a bit at the corners. When the waitress finally graced her with her disinterested gaze, a frown had replaced the smile. She'd recognized Kate.

With all the attention this man got from all the ladies around him, he should have no problem finding a date to take to the Chamber of Commerce dinner party.

"Go for it, lady."

His gaze settled on her.

"What?" Kate asked.

He actually grinned at her. "She's barely legal. I do have my standards."

"I didn't say anything."

His grinned widened. "I like my women a bit older than me."

She wanted to slap that sexy grin off his face. "I'm so happy for you."

"Are you older than me?"

Oh, why didn't he just go back to ignoring her?

"I'm glad to see you two talking again." Esther reached out and touched her son's relaxed bicep. "Good."

Matt frowned. Kate sighed and said, "It's more like a civil argument," the same time he added, "It's more like sarcasm."

Esther pointed her finger at both of them. "I don't care what it is. All I see is two people I care about, talking together."

Kate glanced to the returning waitress, relieved to see their food being placed on the table in the proper places. And, as she watched, the woman paid so much attention to the sensual man beside her no one else seemed to be visible. Did every woman react this way toward him?

"I've got to get back to the office soon."

Carlos looked over his coffee cup at him. "Man, don't fret about the construction. Those men know what they're doing."

"How are the repairs going anyway?" Esther glanced at Carlos, ignoring her son for some unknown reason. "I've known the construction company's owner for ages."

"You have?" Matt said, "I didn't know that." He lifted a large forkful of meatloaf to his mouth, leaving it elevated over the plate. "I guess I've been out of the loop."

"This is good," said Mary, reaching her hand out to touch his raised arm. "I'm glad we decided to eat here."

Jealousy, Kate thought. How can I possibly be jealous over Mary's simple touch? Lifting up her head to stare at the small Hispanic woman, the truth leaped clear into her mind. No, Kate couldn't be jealous. How could she feel such a strong emotion over a man she barely even liked? The dream image of him standing straight and tall near the foot of her bed, naked and exposed in the brilliant sun sank in her mind. The real thing shifted his weight in the seat, brushing his tight thigh against her stiffening leg. He didn't pull it away from her as quickly this time around.

Dark eyes studied her again as his grin warmed over her flushed face. Could he read her mind? Could he see the aftermath of her erotic daydream written in bright large letters on her forehead?

"I think I know a way to keep Peter's legacy alive." Five people turned their attention to Esther. "Matt can take Kate to the Chamber of Commerce dinner."

"No, I don't think I can go," said Kate quickly.

Esther glanced at her. "The dinner party isn't for a two weeks."

"I have obligations in Seattle."

Esther only grinned. "We'll see."

"Mom?"

Kate watched the woman's hand reach over to squeeze her son's arm. "You need to listen to your

77

mother, Matt. I know what's best for you."

Chapter Six

"I don't think that's such a good idea." Matt leaned away from her as Kate glanced with disbelieving eyes at the older woman. Placing his forkful of meatloaf back on the plate, he refused to look in her direction. "I doubt Kate would want to go to a boring Chamber dinner with me anyway."

"Well, what do you say?"

Kate only looked at his mother, ignoring the glare of anxiety in the man's eyes. He stiffened up next to her as she moved a bit toward him. "I used to go to all kinds of boring parties with my husband. It was important for him to be there, so I went with him. I've had my share of politicians."

"You might like it," said Mary, leaning to look past her husband. "Carlos and I will be there. It'll be a chance to get all dressed up."

Carlos laughed. "Maybe Kate doesn't like to get all dressed up.'

"Every woman likes looking pretty." The small woman slapped at her husband's right arm. "It gives us a chance to go out and spend some of our husband's money."

"Kate doesn't have a husband anymore," Carlos grinned at her. "So how is she going to spend any of his money?"

"She still has all his money though." Matt's dark statement stopped the easygoing banter between the Hispanic couple. "He left it all to her."

"And what's wrong with that? That's the way it should be." His mother glanced at Kate for a brief moment before settling her look onto her son. "She was his wife. When your father died, I got everything he owned. How do you think I could afford to go back to school and move? Without the money he left me, I would've been in trouble. I had no skills at all when I met your father, and he took care of me when we were married. It's the same way with Kate."

Sadness chilled through her heart at the implication of the woman's statement. Did he really think she was so despicable, so conniving? Did he really see her in the same light as the characters she used to play so long ago? Suddenly the thought of doing that television series sat heavy on her heart. Did she really want to go through it all over again?

"Boy, are you going to ask her to the dance or not?" Grace touched the top of her fisted hands with a soft fingertip, patting it before staring at her nephew. "I want you to go to the dinner this year. I want you to honor your uncle's memory."

"I'll go, Aunt Grace." He didn't look at Kate. "But I'll find my own date."

****

Kate's breath heaved as the man moved closer to her, his wide chest pressing hard into her. Her breasts settled softly against his naked skin, her bare back pressed into the roughness of the front door of his mother's house. Trapped, naked, she was helpless as his large hands caressed up the side of her full hips and tiny waist, settling in an arrogant way to capture her upright breasts. He stood back from her and glared hot fiery eyes up and down the soft contours of her naked body. He stepped a few more steps backward and he was naked too, alive with lustful energy, hard with desire.

"Matt," she pleaded, "Don't leave me like this."

"You've made a fool of me."

"No, I want you to love me."

"No, you only want my money. Just like Anna. I thought you were different." Disgust showed clear in his face as he backed further away from her, dressed now in the same dark dress pants and gray button down shirt he'd had on at the café. "And I only want 'Monica'. If you want my money, you'll have to play Monica for me."

"No, I'm not her.'

"You're nothing, Kate."

"Nothing, Kate." Bruce walked into the room and he watched Matt nod as if in agreement with him. "I even waited until we were married before I made love to you. Oh, what a disappointment that turned out to be. But, Matt, you must admit she's a fine actress."

"Yes, she almost got an award."

"But reality is something so very different, so very disappointing to me as a husband and to you as a lover."

"Very disappointing." Matt glared at her. "With a body like that, you would think she would know how to satisfy a man."

Jerking awake, Kate pushed the wet sheets from her sweaty body. It was another dream, only a dream. She wasn't standing naked totally unsatisfied after being with Matt, and her deceased husband wasn't all of a sudden alive again to haunt her. No, it was only a dream. A horrible nightmare that spoke truths she didn't want to think about right now. Different from the others concerning this man, this one left her feeling uneasy and unfulfilled instead of aching with hot desire.

And this time Bruce had wandered into the dream. Why had she dreamed of her dead husband?

Shaking away the lingering feelings, she leaped from her bed and raced into the bathroom. The mirror reflected the image of a sexy, beautiful woman with sad blue eyes and short messy blonde hair, yet it didn't show the ugly turmoil fighting inside her heart. It didn't show the normal human desire of a woman needing to be loved and cared for by a complete man.

Because she wasn't a normal woman, she sensed. A tear fell from her eyes as she sank onto the cool tile floor of the dark bathroom, followed by another and another until the floodgates opened and she crawled into a tight position against the rough wall.

No, she wasn't a real woman at all. She hadn't felt like a real woman since doing "Midnight Revenge;" since bringing to life that damn character. Time passed as she sat on the floor, curled up in a ball. Enough time for her tears to dry up and her heart to settle down. Time for her mind to draw back on the truth of her unfulfilling life. Her toughness came in slow waves, rescuing her once again from the brink of despair, and she dragged her body up and out of the bathroom.

It was only a dream. A different one, but still just a dream. And it didn't matter if this nighttime vision hurt her more than the others; it was still only a stupid dream. It meant nothing. Nothing.

But as she lay down on the bed and pulled the crisp white sheet over her trembling body, the emotions formed by the nightmare laid down with her, threatening to destroy her ego completely.

Sleep came slowly.

Thankfully Kate's nightmare didn't return, and around nine that morning she awakened from her troubled sleep. Stretching her arms ceiling-ward, she shook away the lingering fog and stepped toward the bathroom. The effects of the intense reaction showed in the dark under-eye shadows and the fogginess enveloping her mind, but she seemed all right. Fingers combing her hair, she finished the morning routine in record time before grabbing a short silk robe and walking into the kitchen.

The dream wasn't real, but Matt's continuing accusation was too factual to ignore anymore. She needed to find out exactly why her assistant sent him the script instead of Erin. His dislike of everything to do with television seemed obsessive, so getting her assistant's side of the story was necessary for her peace of mind. That Anna must have really hurt him. And his mother wasn't helping the issue. If Esther had her say, he'd just hand over the money for the show to her. If his mother had her way, they'd be married with three kids by now.

Blocking out that sweet image, she picked up the phone and dialed a familiar number. She needed to talk to someone who didn't know Matthew Hunter or his conniving mother. And hearing Dana's caring voice would be good for her psyche too. Her ego could use a boost after the past few days. Dana understood her situation, was the only one who knew the whole truth of her marriage.

Cold water poured into the coffee maker a few minutes later as she waited for the receptionist to answer the phone.

"Williams, William, Gay, & Brown," the young girl said. "How may I direct your call?"

"Hi, this is Mrs. Williams." Ignoring the grinning hello from the cheerful receptionist, she said, "Could you connect me to Dana, please?"

"Yes, I'll do that now. Will you hold please?"

A moment later, her assistant's friendly voice came on the line. "Kate, I'm sorry I wasn't in the office when you called yesterday. It's been a zoo here since you left." Inhaling a loud breath, Dana continued, "How's your vacation? Meet any good-looking guys yet? Getting any sun? It's been raining like crazy here the last week or so."

The load lifted from Kate's shoulders as she listened to her friend's questions in the order remembered. "To answer your many questions—things are going well, no, and a little bit." A nail-screeching sound leaped through the phone line, forcing Kate to move the phone an inch away from her ear.

"No to which question—meeting a new guy or getting some sun?"

"Well..." Matt's rugged face and overpowering body came to mind, and she pushed it back quickly. "To both, I guess. But I did lay out a few days since arriving here."

"You aren't holding anything back on me, are you?"

"No." Hating fibbing to her best friend, Kate spread her hands on the kitchen window and watched as the man disturbing her mind and fleeting though her thoughts stepped from the back of the house next door. "I'm not holding anything back. I haven't met anyone even remotely interesting."

When Matt swept his glance over toward the uncovered kitchen window, she admitted to her own lie. Wanting to or not, this man interested her like no man in a long time.

And that's exactly why she needed to keep from him.

"Kate, why did you call? Do you need me to send you something?" Switching to professional mode, her assistant said her name one more time. "Do you need me to send you anything?"

"Oh, yes."

"Wait, before I forget, I sent that script in an attachment to that new email addy you gave me."

"I didn't give you a new address."

"You didn't?" a sigh sounded clear to Kate. "Hold on for a second and I'll check my records." A moment later, Dana told her the new address. "You told me in the message you sent to me earlier this week to send the script revisions to this addy. I thought it was Erin's, so I didn't see any harm in doing it. What happened? Did you receive the script?"

"Something like that."

"Something like what?"

Silence greeted Kate's loud exhaled breath; Matt

had been right after all.

"What's going on? Who got the revision if you didn't receive them?"

"Don't worry about it, Dana." Before her assistant could say another word, she made a necessary decision. Matt already thought she was after his money, might as well find out all she could about his company. "If I give you a few names, could you get information for me? Discreetly, I mean?"

"Of course." Hearing a few clicks on the keyboard, her assistant asked, "What are the names?"

"The first is Matthew Hunter." Waiting for the clicking to stop, she added, "And the second is a company named TopNotch. It's a protection type-company with bodyguards, security, that sort of thing. Hunter is the owner."

"I'll find out what I can about them." The keyboard clicked in the silence of the phone again, and Kate waited for her friend's next question. Her assistant always had a next question. "Why do you need to know about this guy and his company?"

"It's where you sent the script."

"What?"

"I want to find out more about both the owner and the company."

"Oh, baby!" Dana's excitement stopped Kate from giving her the next assignment. "My computer just hit on TopNotch's website. That Matt guy is hot stuff. Have you met him?"

"He's nice on the eyes, but that's where the niceness ends."

"Oh, you *have* been holding out on me."

"I've seen better looking men."

"Tell me where, and I'll be there by morning." She groaned. "Even in my wildest dreams I couldn't come up with someone that hot."

"So you'll get me the information I asked for?" Kate said, ignoring her outrageous comment. "And will you send me a copy of my speaking engagements for the rest of June and the first week of July?"

"Going to stay beyond your two weeks in California?"

"I'm thinking about it."

"Good for you." Typing noises clicked softly through the silence. "I have a thought. Why don't you do that sex-starved body of yours a favor and get to know that Matt better? I bet you he could get you to forget...everything. It's about time you started dating again."

"Erin is missing."

"What?" The squeak grinding in the phone line told her Dana had jerked up out of her chair. "Erin's missing? What do you mean she's missing? Where is she?"

"She's missing." Kate leaned against the kitchen counter, studying the almost full coffee pot. "I don't know where she is. Well, she's not actually missing. She e-mailed me a couple of times during the week but—" Not wanting to mention her marriage, Kate added, "I haven't heard anything new in a few days."

"Are you all right?"

"Yes." The sudden image of a rugged face surrounded by soft dark-blond hair settled deep in her mind as naked as he'd been in her dreams. Was he truly that delicious looking in real life? "I'd be better if Erin was here with me. Things have been getting to me lately."

"You'll be fine."

"I just need to talk to her."

"Well, you could always talk to me."

Kate sighed before shaking the sadness away and standing up straight near the finished coffee. She pushed at the feeling and reached for a white cup sitting in the dish drainer. "Could you e-mail that schedule to me today sometime? I'm not in any hurry, but I'd like to see if I can cancel some of my appearances."

"The schedule wasn't too full because of your vacation, but let me check." Kate grabbed the coffee pot and poured the steamy liquid into her cup. "Here we go. It says here you only have two seminars scheduled for the rest of June and early July."

"Do you think I could cancel them? Or postpone? Reschedule?"

"One is scheduled for next week here in Seattle; the other one is in the second week of July in Chicago."

"See what you can do about them, won't you?"

"I might be able to cancel the one in July." Her voice sounded strained. "That was a tentative one anyway, but the first, I'm not sure if I can get you out of that one. It's next weekend."

"That'll be all right. If I have to go, I'll go from here and return here." Grabbing her cup, she stared into the dark liquid. "Let me know what you can do as soon as possible, and thank you."

"Sure, anytime." Silence, louder than planes landing at the nearby airfield, set Kate's stomach in knots. Her friend would not let this opportunity go. "Oh, and Kate, you know what I said about that sexy guy? I still think you should take a chance on him."

"He's not interested in me."

"You brought to life one of the sexiest characters of the last decade, how could he not be interested in you?"

"But I'm not that character." Placing the phone down on its cradle without saying good-bye, she stared into the swirled coffee. "If I was her, things would be so much easier."

Chapter Seven

Kate woke early the next morning, a strange fear-like feeling slicing through her entire being. She dragged in a deep breath and stood from the bed, listening for the pounding that had interrupted her dream.

The voice from her dream whispered loud in her brain.

Matt's voice.

When only silence greeted her stilled body, she sat back down at the foot of the bed and sighed. Another dream about that man. And this time the dream felt so real she heard his voice in the room around her, and sensed his very presence. So real she could still feel the touch of his hands running over the naked skin of her back.

Thankfully, Bruce hadn't sneaked into this dream.

Maybe Dana was right, she thought as she cradled her head in her hands. Only a sex-starved woman would be wishing to go back to sleep so she could finish dreaming, only a hungry woman heard lusty non-existent voices yelling out her name.

"Kate, open the door."

Damn, but she had a vibrant imagination.

"Damn it, Kate."

Pounding continued to wrack at the wood of the front door, punctuating each slam in time with his words. She jerked her head from the pillow and listened for a long second before leaping out of the bed and racing to the living room.

She wasn't dreaming.

"If you don't answer right now, I swear I'm going to break down the door."

"No!"

"Kate."

Stopping by the door, she looked down at her short baseball-style pajamas and froze. Oh, dear Lord, she couldn't open the door dressed like this, after that sensuous dream about her alone with him.

"Are you all right?" he asked.

The pounding stopped. Silence settled on the other side of the doorway for a moment before a hard push slammed into the wood, rattling it against its weakening hinges. Leaping away, she breathed in an anxious gasp and screamed his name. Another burst of running footsteps hammered the man against the door, sending her flying a foot closer to the white sofa.

"Stop, Matt."

The impact of his large frame hitting for a third time into the door splintered it from its framework, directing tiny cracks shooting out from the edges of the weak door. Why was Matt trying to break down the door anyway? What was wrong with him?

She raced to the door and yelled out his name. Unlocking it, she said, "I'm opening the door."

He rushed in as soon as it opened wide enough for his large body to squeeze through, and searched with fearful eyes around the dim room. The early morning sunlight shined on the slightly angry, slightly frightened expression on his face when he turned to stare at her for a few intense seconds. As his glance slid over her revealing pajamas his expression changed to a hungrier, darker one.

"You're not hurt."

"Why would I be hurt?" She closed the door before stepping past him and settling into the corner of the sofa, drawing up her legs near to her chest. "I was asleep."

"I just got phone call from someone, who said

you were in danger." His legs seemed to weaken as he dropped into the chair opposite her. "I came running right over here."

"Oh." Her own phone caller came to mind. "Was the person whispering?"

"Yes, I could barely hear her." Straightening in the chair, he leaned toward her and stared. "How did you know the person whispered?"

"I got a whispery phone call too."

"The one telling you Mom was in danger?" She only nodded. "I guess you must have been telling the truth about that."

She only nodded again.

"Look, what did you expect me to think?" His hand reached out to her, one finger caressing her bare calf. She shivered at the brief touch, a memory of her dream playing havoc with reality. "I came over expecting to find a stalker messing with my mother, and I catch you hiding in my old bedroom closet."

"You were really worried about your mother?"

"Of course I was worried." He placed his hands on his lap. "Grace called me, remember?"

"And now you're worried about me."

"Yes."

"Oh." Pulling her legs closer to her middle, she wrapped her arms tighter around them. A brief grin formed over his mouth at her defensive position before he stood from the chair and sat next to her trembling body.

"I think my mother and aunt are behind all these calls."

Kate smiled softly. "It's pretty obvious."

"Does it bother you?"

She didn't know what to say to that. "They're harmless calls." She wrapped her arms tighter around her suddenly chilled legs, and glanced down at her stiff fingers.

"You need to relax."

"I'm relaxed."

"I'm not planning on touching you again." The corners of his mouth uplifted into a gentle grin, not believing her simple statement. "As least I don't plan on touching you right now, so you don't need to be so uptight."

"I'm not uptight."

He actually laughed.

"And why shouldn't I be uptight?" Stretching out her legs to their full length, she stood up and glared down at his relaxed form. "You'd be uptight too if someone came pounding on your door at four in the morning. I hope you know you're going to have to pay to fix it."

"It's five."

"What?"

"It's five in the morning, not four." His silvery gray eyes stole down her front, lingering on her long legs for a hot minute before caressing back up her trembling upper body to her blushing face. She didn't need to see her reaction; she knew. "Do you always look this...good in the morning?"

Refusing to cover up her tightening reaction to his compliment, she stood taller and walked out of the living room. How dare he look at her like that? Only a few days ago he'd been accusing her of trying to use this same body for her own evil purposes, implying only yesterday about her *taking* her husband's money.

"You better change into something a bit less revealing." His statement sounded like a command, sounded like he planned on staying for a while. Invited or not. "I'll make some coffee."

"I appreciate you caring, but I'm going back to bed."

His voice deepened. "If you're not out of that room and in this kitchen by the time this coffee's done, I'll come and get you."

"Good-bye, Matt."

"Don't play games with me, Kate." A dangerous

hint of anger darkened around his playful words. "I always win."

Oh no, you won't this time, Matthew Hunter. But instead of climbing back into her still warm bed, she changed into a pair of white shorts and a bright yellow top and finger combed her short hair into a smooth mess. Without glancing in the mirror, she walked from the bedroom and into the kitchen a mere two minutes later.

Why take the chance on him actually following through on his threat?

A look of triumph fleeted quickly across his rugged face when she stepped into the room and sat.

"You look nice."

"Thank you." If he wanted to play a game, she would play a game. "You look nice too."

And he did look fine right now. Unshaved and dressed in a pair of faded old blue jean shorts and a size-too-small T-shirt, he sent her heart speeding wildly beneath her breasts. The shirt enhanced the powerful muscles of his upper body to perfection, and those legs. Tanned and strong, the thought of feeling those light-haired legs sliding against her lower body made her melt.

Just like in her dreams. "I've never seen you looking better."

"You like ragged, unshaven men, do you?"

"Even ragged and unshaved, you still look better than a lot of men."

"This is my nighttime look." Eyes sparkling with dark highlights, he grinned, "Like it?"

"Oh." Surprise flicked through her at his confession. "Really? I would think a man like you would sleep nude."

"I do," his grin widened, "when I'm with a woman."

"Of course."

He stared into her eyes, deep into her eyes. "Interested, Kate?"

Taken aback, she stood from the table and moved to the coffee maker. "I drink my coffee with milk. What would you like?"

"I like mine black."

When the beeping sound sang from the machine, she poured the black liquid into the two cups sitting near it. She poured a generous amount of fresh milk into hers and stirred it before grabbing both cups.

"My Dad used to drink his coffee black," Matt said taking the cup from her. "I think that's why I drink it black now."

"Both my parents drink their coffee with cream," she said in relief as she settled down into the chair. She would rather talk about coffee than wonder what he looked like naked in bed. Day dreaming when she was alone was bad enough. "All five of my brothers drink it black."

"Yeah, that's right. You did have five brothers."

"How did you know that?" She stared at him. "Did Erin tell you?"

He glanced at his cup for a moment. "They're all older than you."

"They are good guys though."

"It must have been hard growing up with five older brothers." He leaned into the table, encircling his fingers around the hot cup. "I bet with all those brothers around you had a hard time dating."

She laughed. "Most boys gave up pretty quickly after meeting my brothers. It used to drive me crazy."

"Most boys?"

"There were a few who stood up to them."

"Thought they were tough, did they?"

"Yes, I learned on my own how to get past my brothers' protectiveness." She took a small sip of the coffee. "I think dealing with their overbearing attitude toward me was the real beginning of my acting career."

"They were concerned for you." His answer

surprised her. "If I had sisters, I would've acted the same way."

"If I had only one brother, I would've accepted the behavior. But five are enough to drive even the sweetest girl to do the wrong thing."

"And you did the wrong thing?"

"I was sixteen." She smiled warm, remembering that time with delight. "I was still in high school when I made love for the first time."

"Mine was with the sister of my best friend in high school." His mouth widened into a bright smile. "I met her about a year after my Dad died, but we didn't start dating until I turned sixteen."

"That must have been hard for you."

"I survived."

"Was your dad in security too?" She asked in the sudden silence. "Was he a bodyguard like you?"

"He worked with my uncle."

"Oh." She grinned, catching his quick lowering glance. "You mean he was rich like your uncle?"

When he didn't respond, she looked up and stared into his eyes. Anger darkened their color, deepening the soft gray a hard black. What had she said to bring back that suspicious look again?

"I need to be going soon."

"You don't need to leave, Matt."

"Yes, I do," he whispered.

"Do you need to leave because of me?"

His gaze moved over her face. His suspicion sent her heart racing in sudden annoyance, releasing her anger. "I'm glad you're all right," he said.

"I *was* fine." She stood and leaned into his stiffening body. "Until you remembered that I'm a conniving bitch who is after your damn money."

His glare spoke volumes; no words needed to be said. But the last words needed to be spoken to break up the easy feeling they'd been sharing the last half-hour or so. She sensed this with her whole being.

"If you didn't want me to think of you that way, you wouldn't have sent me that script. You wouldn't have talked to that producer. You wouldn't have lied to me about Erin."

"What?" Her hot gaze focused on his clamped hands, anger rising up to burn her. "I haven't lied to you about anything, especially about Erin."

"Erin told me about the television series before you arrived in California, but she neglected to tell me about you." She moved back away from him as he stood, trapping her bottom into the edge of the counter. "I already told *her* that I wasn't interested in sponsoring the series, now I'm telling *you* the same thing."

"Why would she ask you to do anything? We haven't even decided to do the pilot episode yet."

"It's one lie after another with you, isn't it? I know you decided to do the series a while back. Erin told me." Hot fire charged out of his accusing eyes, pushing her back into the corner of the counter. "And when I told Erin I didn't want to get involved in it, she decided to bring you into the picture to try to convince me to change my mind."

"You're so wrong."

"And you could do it too," he whispered, "Erin knew you could."

Her temper pulled her up and away from the counter and into his stone-hard body. He tightened at her touch but didn't pull away. Even now, his nearness affected her reasoning power; even now she burned.

"That's why she sent for you."

"Do you think you're the only person worth millions?"

He didn't back from her, didn't pull her forward to him. He only stared deep into her eyes, breezing warm mint into her senses.

"I'm also worth millions of dollars, Mr. Hunter. I was worth millions before I married my husband,

and I'm worth more now." Standing up even taller, she placed her hand against the pronounced abdominal muscles stretching the shirt tight. "I don't *need* your money; I don't *want* your money."

"Yes, Katherine, you are worth more now." He moved from her frozen frame and added, "After all every one knows your deceased *older* husband was worth billions."

Chapter Eight

Kate froze against the corner of the counter. The sharp edges bit into her left hip, but she ignored it as she watched the accusing man sit down. When he picked up his cup as if nothing had happened, she exploded, "How dare you say such a thing to me?"

"If the truth hurts," he said, "it's not my fault. I only stated the facts."

"The facts?"

His hand clamped around his cup, reddening the knuckles. "He *was* fifteen years older than you."

"How am I supposed to respond to that? I was twenty-six when we married; he was forty-one."

"And he wasn't even fifty when he died."

She clutched her hands into fists, gulping in one deep breath after another. "I see that you've kept up with the classier newspapers and magazines."

"Your name still has value."

"Katherine Adams has value." She stepped toward him, stopping a bare six inches from him. "Kate Williams isn't that person."

"Did you love him?" A blank look pierced clear to her soul. "Those tabloids may be trash, but there is always a germ of truth in the stories."

"Not always truth." Did she love Bruce? How could she love someone who barely could stand touching her? She didn't want to think of it now; not with this perceptive man staring hard at her. He would misread her expression, assuming it was her decision to move into separate bedrooms a month after their second anniversary. "Not always."

He snaked his hand out and touched her face,

lifting it up to check into her eyes.

Something soft and reassuring lightened in his glance, in the gentleness of his touch, yet it scared her. "Don't touch me like that."

"I'm sorry," he said, allowing his fingers to smooth over her skin.

"You're sorry." She jerked away and sank into one of the chairs. "I should never have come to California."

He didn't say a word.

"When Erin started talking about this wonderful script, I should've followed my first impulse and told her I wasn't interested in it."

"Kate, you—"

Interrupting his denial, she looked over her cup. "I know you think I've said yes to the series. You think I'm a secret weapon meant to weaken you, but I'm not. I'm just a confused woman who is tired of living a dispassionate life."

"Erin knew how I felt about you when I was young."

She jerked toward him. "What do you mean by that?"

"I…was a fan."

"Oh." She gulped as she watched his hard chiseled face blush a light pink. If she weren't so attuned to his features, she would've missed his embarrassment. "I remembered someone saying you'd seen my movies."

He actually grinned. "I thought you walked on water."

"You did?"

He smiled softly. "When the newspaper stated you were leaving the business to get married, I was hurt."

Kate didn't quite believe him. "Tomorrow would've been my eleventh anniversary. June 21st."

Matt glanced at her before settling his intense gaze on his cup. "I'm sorry, Kate. I don't know why I said that about your marriage."

"Some people want to believe the worst of everyone."

"But I'm not that way." He reached over and lightly touched her fist. She didn't pull away this time. "I've been a target of those people too. I know how damaging their half-truths can be."

"Emily told me you're...different now." The warmth of friendship lingered around them. Although she figured it was only a temporary thing, she'd decided to enjoy it. "I got the impression she knew you."

"Yes." He relaxed into his chair, loosening his hold on his cup. "I grew up here. "Well, not really grew up. I was fourteen when we moved to this town. After my father died."

Silence lingered for a moment. "How did he die?"

Sadness moistened his eyes, and he lowered his head to the table. When he raised his head, slight guilt mixed with his grief. "My dad was guarding a woman who was having trouble with her boss. She'd caught him doing something illegal, but I'm not sure what." Glancing at his large hands, he whispered, "TopNotch Security was hired to protect her, and my dad was assigned her case. On the day of the trial, my dad was driving her to the courthouse. Neither one of them made it."

"Your dad died protecting this woman?"

He only nodded.

"Your father was a hero."

"Yes." He drew her hand into his, lengthening his fingers to wrap around hers. She held on tight, liking the feel of his slightly callused palm and long, strong fingers. "I've never told anyone that story."

"You should be proud of him."

"At the time, I was only angry."

His thumb moved in slow circles over the surface of her skin. Surging heat pooled in her at his innocent stroke, leaving her yearning for something deeper, something more real. Bruce had never touched her like this, leaving her aching for more.

"I was pissed.

"You were fourteen." She tightened her grip and placed her other hand on top their entwined fingers. "I remember when my brothers were teenagers."

"Oh," he said, "your poor mother."

She laughed at his expression, grabbing the new conversation with relish. "My mom was fine with it, but not my dad." She laughed at his expression. "The poor man was furious most of the time. By the time I was a teenager, he'd accepted that he couldn't fix everything."

"I doubt he gave his only daughter much freedom."

"Oh, don't get me wrong. He was a good dad."

"So you didn't have to *act* around him?"

She frowned at his question, at the emphasis placed on the word *act*.

"He was a wonderful father; always there for me. I didn't need to act around him. He was my biggest fan, and he still is."

Matt lifted their tangled hands and brought them to his lips. Warm mist-like air breezed over her knuckles as he slid his lips over her delicate skin, melting her at his simple touch.

The intense look in his eyes stopped her next words. As Kate watched him, his expression tightened with a question before softening with his own answer. "Would you go out to dinner with me tonight?"

"Tonight?"

"Yes."

"I don't…"

Another decision relaxed his grip on her hand, and he turned it upwards to trace a finger along her palm. "I want to get to know you better."

"Why?"

"I'm not going to hurt you, Kate." Her shocked

expression startled him. "I just want to have dinner with you."

Oh, Kate wanted to say yes. She so desperately wanted to say yes. "I can't."

"Why?"

"I just can't go out with you."

"Kate, if I promise not to talk about your husband or the television series, will you go out with me?"

She didn't know what to say.

"And I promise I'll be better dressed. What do you say?"

When she realized she'd go out with him even if he showed up in old jeans and ragged t-shirt, she grinned. "Do you promise not to mention my past or Erin or the television series or Bruce?"

He laughed. "Doesn't leave us much to talk about."

Oh, was she making a mistake?

"But I promise," he said.

"Okay, I'll love to go out with you tonight."

****

Completely, totally insane, Matt thought. He had to be crazy to ask that woman to go to dinner with him. What had gotten into him this morning? He glanced down at his laptop, mesmerized by the little green, red, and blue boxes slowly twisting and turning into circles and spheres.

Insanity, he thought. Yet the way she'd looked with those long legs and that sleep shapely body barely concealed by the filmy material of her short pajamas stopped his mind from functioning. He wanted to pull her to him and kiss those glistening lips of hers, to feel that lightly tanned skin pressed into him.

"Get out of my head, sexy lady."

Rummaging through the papers covering the top of the hotel's desk, he picked up the one he wanted. Carlos had read this script, and loved it. His wife had read it, and cried. He'd promised her he'd read it too. So far he'd only picked it up and put it back down again.

Too soon, he thought, for him to make this decision. He would eventually; he knew he would read it soon. Just like he knew he'd be lying next to Kate, cradling her body against his.

A soft knock on the door filtered through his decision, and a picture of a leggy blonde flashed briefly in his mind, the sweet soothing sound of her sexy voice dripping sugar.

But, when he opened the door, the image faded. "What are you doing here, Anna?"

"Is that any way to greet your ex-lover?" Brown thick hair fell from her upturned head, swinging soft over her right shoulder. "Are you going to invite me in?"

"There's no need for that."

"I have the ring."

"I broke the engagement," he said. "Keep it."

"Matt, I...made a mistake with...that man." She reached to touch him. He pushed her raised hand away and backed to the bed. "I guess I'm not allowed to make mistakes."

"I caught you in bed with another man." Hurt formed the words but he didn't feel any pain. "If you need me to forgive you then I'll forgive you, but it doesn't matter to me anymore."

"Matt, I thought we could—"

"I've nothing more to say to you." He'd hurt deeply when he'd caught her, in his bed, with that director. Now he just felt relief that he'd found out about her before making the biggest mistake of his life. "If you want to give me back the ring, set it on the dresser and leave. I have nothing more to say to you."

Anna stood so quiet now he could hear the swishing of her long skirt rubbing against her bare legs. As she turned to the dresser, she said, "You've found someone else."

Kate, he thought before quickly forcing her image away. "No."

"For a while, I was thinking you'd fallen for Erin." She pushed the folders around the dresser. She grasped the script of "Two Sisters" in her tight fingers when she twisted to face him, a quick glimpse of hatred flashing in her eyes. "Is this Erin's second chance?"

He stared at the papers.

"Or do you have it because of *Katherine Adams*?"

"She likes to be called Kate now."

Her laughter shot out like a bullet from a high-powered rifle, hitting him directly in the center of his heart. "And here I thought you were an intelligent man."

Matt froze at her insult, at the implication of her words. "You're here to give me back my ring, remember? I think you need to place the box on the bed and leave."

"Does the truth hurt you, baby?"

"Anna." Her laughter stopped as quickly as it'd started, bringing a loud silence to the chilled room. "You may see her as only Kate, but inside she's still the same woman who brought to life characters like Monica in movies like *Midnight Revenge*. And don't try to deny what character I'm talking about. You did more than just provide me with some amazing sex after mentioning that particular movie."

Yes, he remembered in a weak moment mentioning about having a crush on a certain actress, but he'd never mentioned any names.

"I always thought it was Erin." Her conniving smile sickened his stomach, but he swallowed down the burning taste. "But now I think maybe I guessed wrong."

"Just leave, Anna."

"I'll be leaving, baby." She threw the script on the neat bed and stepped out the door. "Maybe you should read that."

"I said leave.'"

She laughed soft this time. "She wants to get back into acting."

"That doesn't matter to me." And he sensed the truth of his words. He would read the script; he would sponsor the series. "Her past doesn't matter."

"Do you really believe that?" she asked before closing the door behind her.

Does her past matter? Did his own matter? He glanced down at the spilled pages lying on the bed. Is she only using me to get back to the person she used to be?

"No."

Retrieving the pages from the bed, he placed them in one of the bottom drawers of the dresser. Out of sight, out of mind, he thought. He wanted to read it, but until he figured out what the sexy lady was after, he'd keep it tucked away.

Chapter Nine

When Kate opened the door at exactly five o'clock that evening, she froze at the sight of him, dragging in a long startled breath. Matt looked better in his gray Armani suit than any male had the right to look. The gray enhanced the soft blonde color of his hair to perfection; the crisp white silk shirt and tan tie pulled the whole outfit together to show his wealth and elegance.

Suddenly she was glad she decided to wear one of her more expensive sundresses. "Hi," she said, "You look nice."

"And you look lovely." His gaze traveled over her softly clad figure, moving over the revealing red material of her dress with interest. The sparkle in his bright eyes spoke to her of a more dangerous man now, a different one, a determined one. His new determination frightened her, sending her heart pounding out of her control. "You look great in red."

"Thank you."

Trying on every one of her new dresses was the right thing to do, she thought. And red did do something for her. Short, a few inches above her knees, the dress sank low in the front and even lower in the back. With a single halter tie keeping it from falling from her naked breasts, she felt both wicked and beautiful. At the look in his scorching silvery eyes, she figured he saw her much in the same way tonight. His glance moved slowly, sensually down the length of her long, slightly tanned legs before caressing up her body to settle on her naturally made-up face.

"Yeah, red definitely is your color."

Pulling at the short skirt, she said, "It's a little bit short, don't you think?"

Disbelief rolled his eyes upward as a sudden laugh roared from deep in his throat. "You're truly one of a kind."

For once she accepted his words as the compliment they were meant to be, and a flirty kind of mood came over her with such abruptness it scared her. But why not enjoy this man's company today? Why not try to renew the hint of friendship that had surrounded them this morning? It would be better than fighting with him all the time.

And she was so damn tired of fighting with this man.

"Lady, you would look sexy in a trash bag."

"Oh." He frightened her, but he also filled her with emotions she hadn't felt in a long time. "I do?"

"You should know that."

Today she did. Right now, with this man looking at her like he wanted to devour her from the tips of her red painted toes to the edges of her soft blonde hair flashing around her cheekbones, she felt like the beautiful actress she used to be before life messed with her.

"I'm beginning to believe that." And with the words spoken out loud, with the satisfied look lingering in his eyes at her statement, she started to feel the belief race through her system. "Are you ready to go?"

"Yes," he said.

"So where are we going?"

"There's a nice place in Jackson Square where we can sit outside and enjoy the weather." He took hold of her arm and directed her to the BMW. "It has a great view of the shops."

"That sounds nice."

He grinned. "And maybe, if they're people wandering in and out of the shops, we might actually be able to talk without yelling at each other."

She laughed.

"But what we'll talk about I'm not sure." Opening the car door, he waited for her to slip inside before closing it and going around to the driver's side. "I guess I'll just have to bore you by talking about myself and my business."

"That'll be fine." She smiled toward him as he backed out of the driveway. "And, thank you for respecting my wishes."

"It's only temporary." His intense gaze confused her, frightened her in a way she didn't quite understand. She trembled. "I'm going to want to find out all I can about you sometime."

"Why?"

He shook his head at her question. "You really are unique, Katie." His laugh floated to her in the slight breeze of the warm California wind, heating her from the inside out. "You're the only woman I've ever met who didn't realize how sexy and beautiful she truly is."

Pleased by his compliment, she said, "Thank you."

His laughter intensified as he pulled into the filled parking lot and stopped the car. "Here we are." He grabbed her smooth elbow and turned her to the opening of the lively building.

Still smiling, she walked through the flowered lined door and stopped to take in her surroundings in the dimly lit space. Tiny circular tables made for two sat around the café with high softly padded chairs beside them. A few couples sat close together at the romantic settings, not looking up as they moved through the room to an empty table. The whole atmosphere of the restaurant reminded her of the cafés Bruce had taken her to on their honeymoon to Europe. "This is nice."

"Yes, I like it here." He couldn't seem to stop

smiling, she thought.

"It's my aunt's favorite restaurant. But my mom was the one who suggested I take you here tonight."

"I can hear her now." She smiled as she changed her facial expression, mimicking his mother's tone and cadence to a near perfect pitch. "It serves the best food in the whole town, and the view is breathless."

"That sounds just like her." Surprise sounded in his voice, and his laughter roared in the air around them. The surrounding diners glanced toward their table, grinning at his exuberance. "You are a good actress."

"Some people are easier to mimic than others." Slipping into the chair he'd pulled out for her, she watched as he sat on the opposite side of the oval table—set for two, an intimate setting all arranged by his mother and aunt, no doubt. "Your mother has a unique way of saying things. And Grace—" Changing her tone again, she said, "Boy, you couldn't be more foolish if you tried."

He roared again, reaching out to touch the tip of her nose. "You're too much."

"I'm normal." She smiled and pulled his hand down, entwining her fingers with his. His eyes widened at her unexpected touch. "It's your conniving mother and crazy aunt who are too much."

"Crazy as two foxes." The gray of his eyes changed into bright sparkling lights as he gazed at her, sending her heart spinning out of control. No desire shined in his eyes, no lust. Yet the look stopped needed breath from entering her lungs. "Those two have been trying to hook me up with available females for years. Mom has been clear about what she wants from me, but until now I wasn't...."

"You mean grandchildren?"

His look intensified again, now shining forth with a hot glare of desire. "Now, I'm beginning to see her side of things. I think that's why I..."

A warm ache settled in the pit of her stomach. "So, do you ever plan on giving her any grandchildren?"

"I never really thought about it before."

She sighed as his hot glance slide down to their entangled fingers, sighing again when his thumb moved over the skin of her relaxed hand. She tightened up at his gentle touch, pent up breath escaping her lungs before she forced her body to calm down. His now blank look moved once more to her face, studying her with probing eyes. *What are you thinking? Are you seeing Anna in your mind now?* She didn't want him remembering his ex when they were in this intimate place.

"Hey, Matt." A loud boisterous man slammed two filled glasses of iced tea on the table. He nodded toward her. "How're things going with you? Where are the ladies?"

"Why do you assume my mom and aunt are with me tonight?"

"Are you telling me you're back in circulation?" His open look settled on her for a brief moment, taking her all in with that one glance. "Things are looking up for you. This one is even better than the last."

She should've been upset and angry at his comments. So why wasn't she feeling more offended? "I'm not...I'm not better."

"Talkative one, isn't she?"

At this statement, she did let her temper go. "I'll have you know I'm a licensed and practicing attorney from Seattle, and I *can* articulate quite well."

"Wow, down baby," the man said, raising his hands toward the ceiling. "I'm sorry for speaking out of turn."

"Kate can hold her own, George."

"Kate, huh?" His glance swung down her one

more time while he told them the specials of the day. "You sure do look familiar."

Unease entered her mind, and she looked down to their still entwined hands.

"Oh, well," he said, "Gorgeous is gorgeous. Beautiful women are part of the landscape around this area."

"Not like my Kate," Matt spoke under his breath. "What would you like to eat?"

Did he really just call her 'my Kate'? Staring into his blank face, she decided it was only her imagination. Like in her dreams of them together, he'd always referred to her as 'my Kate'. "Everything sounds so good, why don't you decide for both of us?"

"Is there anything in particular you don't like?"

"Not really," Kate said. "I love seafood."

"I'll get the two of you the assortment plate." The heavy man walked away from the table before either one of them agreed to his suggestion.

"Wow, he's something else."

"Blunt and to the point, yes." Matt looked from the disappearing man, back to her. "But he's a good man. He used to be stationed at Camp Pendleton. He's retired from the military now, and works here a few days a week. He likes getting into people's business."

"The Marine base?" Kate asked.

"Yes, it's not too far from here." He smiled. "He looks out for my mom and aunt when I'm not around."

"You don't live here all the time?"

"I only live here a part of the year." Looking down at their still entwined hands, he sighed gently before releasing the grip. Coldness rushed into her skin to replace the warmth of his touch. "I have to spent a lot of my time in the city for business reasons. But it should be only a few more months until I move here permanently. I'm in town finishing up the remodeling of a small security firm I recently acquired. I plan on moving my headquarters here soon."

Quietness settled around them as she watched him wipe his long fingers down the chilled glass.

"Is that how you made all that money? Buying up small security firms?" The question came out before she had time to stop it. "I mean—"

Blankness filled his face at her question.

"I'm only asking a question, Matt." Slight displeasure lowered the tone of her voice at the presumption she read behind the emptiness in his eyes. "The only reason I'm asking is because I'm interested in knowing more about you, too."

A hint of fire played over the edges of the emptiness for a brief second as his shoulders lifted and back straightened in response to her words.

"We should declare a truce," Kate said.

"Yeah, we should declare a truce." Dazed, the man seemed different from his usual self. Not as domineering, as powerful, as controlling, he seemed off, as if he'd fallen and hit his head against the hard wood floor. Nice in a way, yet she preferred the real Matt. "Yeah, a truce between us would be a nice change."

"If you don't want to talk about TopNotch, I won't ask any more questions."

One of his fingers reached up to lightly trace her lower lip. "We don't need to talk."

"We can talk about—"

"No, we don't talk at all."

"Why?"

"Please, Kate." Gruffness roughened in his voice, a roughness that brought back the real Matt to her. "Your voice—damn but I love your voice."

"You love my voice?" His fingers moved over the fullness of her lower lip, effectively trapping her words inside her mouth. "Matt?"

"Do you know your voice gets all sexy and sultry when you're excited or pissed about something?" His touch traveled from her lip to encircle her chin in a gentle yet firm way. "Do you have any idea how that makes a man feel?"

"My 'Monica' voice," she said lightly, "Yes, I know."

"No, it's not 'Monica's' voice." Pulling her face a bit closer to his lips, he almost touched his mouth to hers. "It's your voice, Katie."

"Hey, that'll be enough of that stuff." George's approach stopped the delicate foreplay before she wanted it to end. Oh, but she wanted to believe he'd heard that sultry breathy voice as her own. "This is a respectable joint—not some dive for couples to make-out."

****

"Stop that Kate," Matt said, soft grin belying his tight words. "It's a nice thought but we're eating dinner now."

"What are you talking about?"

Leaning toward her, he placed his fork on his plate and grabbed her face roughly in both hands. "Tell me you weren't just seeing me naked in your mind."

"No, I was only..." But she couldn't lie. She'd been studying his profile, traveling her glance over the soft blonde hair brushing against the collar of his jacket to the rugged features of his smooth tanned skin.

"Damn, but you are beautiful."

"Matt?"

"I see you naked in my dreams too."

"Do you?" She lifted her hand and touched the place where his skin showed through his shirt. Not traditionally handsome like Bruce, this man had an overwhelming presence. He had the ability to stop her heart with a single scorching look, leaving her aching and breathless with a brief touch. "Do you dream about me too?"

He only stared into her eyes, allowing her to

play around the buttons of his shirt before pulling at her and bringing her lips within an inch of his mouth. "I've been dreaming about you for a long time."

"Really?"

Matt jerked his hands from her face and sat back, leaving her wondering what she'd done to change his mood this time. "We should eat this before it gets cold. You'll like it."

And she did like it. A platter full of white fish, clams, and tiny shrimp mixed with a few hush puppies sat emptied in front of her a mere half-hour later. "I can't believe I ate all that food."

"Didn't I tell you?"

Wiping her mouth with the white linen napkin, Kate picked up her tea and finished it in three long swallows. "I'm glad we decided to go out on this date."

"I am too."

"It's nice not to be fighting," she added.

"Yes."

She placed the empty glass onto the table, moved sideways in her chair and crossed her legs. His glance settled on her swinging foot for a moment before caressing up the length of her naked leg. "I do have nice legs, don't you think?"

"Long, long sexy legs meant to be wrapped around—" He jerked up straight and stared toward the front of the room and spied the large waiter. "I always thought George had a thing for my aunt. His wife died a few years ago, and he'd started looking after her and my mom. Aunt Grace could use another husband."

"Maybe he's interested in your mom," teased Kate. "I mean, she's still a beautiful woman."

He stared at her for a long time. "I doubt if my mom would be interested in him. She's never gotten over my dad."

Sadness whispered in his voice, and she reached

over to cover his lower arm. "That must have been hard for you too, losing your father, I mean."

"I survived." Matt looked away from her, ignoring her unasked question. "It was harder on my mother until she moved here to be near Aunt Grace and Uncle Peter."

"That was good for her." Leaning forward over her crossed knees, she glanced into his lowered face. She tightened her hand on his arm, feeling the muscles bunch under her touch. "But who did you have?"

The dark look burning in his eyes brought her back against the wood of the old chair, and she dropped her hand from him. Her heart pounded as she held his intense stare, spying a vulnerability hiding deep in his feature. Somehow, in some way, that weakness spoke to her. In some way, she sensed she was the reason for the hint of vulnerability shining naked in his eyes.

"I kept a journal."

"And it helped you cope with your father's death?"

His mouth opened as if to say something important before he slammed it shut and stood from the chair, rocking it back on its hind legs in his haste to get away.

Only then, did she look around her and see all the other tables filled with an assortment of male and female characters, all staring at Matt's straight and commanding form in the middle of the room. A few of the men stared aghast at her, a few of the women glared cold eyes in her direction. The usual reaction when people recognized her, lust from the men, hate from the women, stopped her breath in her lungs.

Slipping from her chair, she ignored the people trying to catch her attention and walked behind Matt's impelling figure. Her finger slid down his arm to capture his stiff hand into her warm one before she stepped to the cashier near the front entrance and unzipped her purse. When she reached into the tiny space for her credit card, he stopped her movement and pulled out his wallet. After retrieving his card and placing a five-dollar bill on the table, he reclaimed her hand and stepped with her out of the door.

The heat of the late evening sun warmed the bare skin of her exposed back and slightly tanned legs, laid hot against the top of her head in a sensuous way.

"This was nice, Matt." Trying to pull her hand from his grip at the door of his car, she turned to face him. "I can't get in the car if you won't let go of my hand."

"You're going to the Chamber of Commerce dinner with me, right?"

"Matt, I already...."

"No." Pulling their connected hands behind his back, Kate stepped easily into his inviting body. "You'll go with me."

"Is that a command I'm hearing from you?"

"I want you with me." His mouth brushed over the sun-heated warmth of her short blonde hair, sending a shiver of lust into her middle. Oh, it was so hard to refuse him anything when he acted so domineering, so controlling, so overpowering. Was she so masochistic that she got excited by an overassertive man? Bruce had been this way at times too, and he'd only left her feeling cold. "With you on my arm, all the other guests will be envious of me. I'll be able to get anything I want from them."

Bruce all over again, she thought. "No, I can't go."

"Kate?"

"I won't let anyone use me like that again."

Startled by her angry statement, she felt him step away from her. But he didn't release her hand from behind his back. She moved a half step toward him to keep from hurting her trapped arm, turning sideways so only her hip touched his front. Somehow that positioning was less threatening.

But still his reaction to her nearness was obvious.

"How would I be using you? I would be proud to have you on my arm." He leaned closer to her downward angled face, brushing her temple with his lips. "I would be proud and honored to be escorting 'Katherine Adams' to the party."

"Would you be as honored and proud if I had a different past?"

"You would still be the same person, Kate." He let go of her hand and reached inside his jacket pocket for the car keys. His hands lingered on her shoulders as she settled into the seat. "If I promise not to push you into something you're not ready for, will you go to the dinner with me?"

"Matt, try to understand how I feel about this."

"No." Brushing his hand lightly along the edge of her cheek, he quickly closed the door and raced around the car. Getting behind the wheel, he turned to her. "Look at me."

She did as he asked, without a thought.

"I'm not going to accept a negative answer." He captured her face between his hands and stared into her eyes. "I'm going to win this battle, Kate."

"Do you always get what you want?"

As if in answer, he caressed his fingers over her bottom lip before placing his lips on hers with a soft gentleness that threatened to melt her. The kiss soon changed to a more demanding one, hot and piercing clear to the center of her.

Whispering near her damp lips, he asked, "You're going to the party with me, right?"

As she started to protest his lips fell onto hers once again, a searching snaking tongue playing havoc with her senses. He probed deep into the warm wetness of her mouth, sending protest out of her mind. Caressing his hands over the top of her head, he moved his touch over her bare shoulders. The kiss deepened as he placed his opened palm against the smooth skin of her back, twirling a delicate line of small circles toward the bottom edge of her sundress.

"Go to the party with me, Kate."

This is what it meant to be the seduced instead of the seducer, she thought with suddenness. As his lips rose from hers and his hand moved to clamp the headrest of her seat, she understood why men wanted women like the character 'Monica' so much. She seduced, promised an ending to the aching need pooling into the other's blood, promised a satisfaction of all their most vivid dreams.

"Go to the party with me."

"Yes." She should stay with her first answer, stay with her intended no, but his promise of fulfillment was too powerful to overcome. Kate wanted her aching to end, all of her pain. Just for one night, for one brief encounter, she wanted to feel alive again. "I'll be happy to be your trophy date."

****

Kate second guessed her decision at least twice before they'd arrived in silence at Erin's home. When he'd kissed her good-bye at the door, with the same brief hint of promise he'd unconsciously made earlier, she'd changed her mind back again. While changing out of the way-too-sexy dress into an old pair of jean shorts and a simple T-shirt, she'd changed her mind one more time. But each time she came to the same conclusion for the same reason. He showed her his vulnerable side by telling her about his father and he showed her his domineering side by ordering her to go to the party.

She should be ashamed for being so hot over a man so controlling, yet...since playing that sexy troublemaking woman in her breakout role all the men she'd dated wanted her to be the aggressor.

117

Even after Bruce's death, the few times she'd decided to take a chance with some man, she'd still needed to act like that character 'Monica'.

But Matt—

Did he really want a trophy woman? Someone who would look hot on his arm? Someone all the other men at the party would envy him for? She sensed this small town wasn't filled with former actresses except Erin, and she'd been claimed by her professor.

Was she making a mistake? Before she could change her mind for the fifth time, the phone in the kitchen rang. She pushed the unanswerable question from her and raced into the far room, grabbing the receiver on the second ring.

Hoping to hear Erin's voice, disappointment filled her. "You were with him."

"Who is this?" A familiar female voice, but whose?

"You need to be careful."

"I asked who you are."

"You know me."

Slight fear moved through her system. "But I don't know you."

"Talk to Erin."

"She's…not home now."

Silence lingered so long she thought the caller had disconnected. "When she gets there, ask her about Matt."

"Matt? What about Matt?" A trembling fright clamped her fingers around the phone. "What are you talking about?"

"Check up on him." Silence again before she added, "You're a lawyer. Check up on him."

"How do you know I'm a lawyer?"

"Just check him out."

"Who are you?"

"He's not as he seems." Anger deepened the caller's voice, pulling it past the whisper stage. "He's a user. He promises things in order to get his way, to steal—"

"A user?"

"Ask Erin."

"He used Erin?"

"Got what he wanted from her, got what he wanted from me." The whisper lowered into soft accusation. "And now he wants the same thing from you."

Chapter Ten

Kate woke on Sunday to the sound of hard, rushing rain pounding on the bedroom window, thundering, blowing wind wiping through the trees. The rain was a pleasant change from the hot California sun, and she welcomed it, but still, it frightened her. This rainstorm, with furious wind heaving large drops of water to the thirsty ground, fit her mood. All night long she'd wavered from wanting to go to the Chamber of Commerce dinner with Matt, and not wanting to go. And still confusion lingered in her mind as she sat up straight in her bed.

Lightning flashed, a loud thundering clap that shook her slightly. The storm frightened her, but indecision frightened her more. Even with the memory of the newest whispered warning, she still didn't know what to do.

And it was all that man's fault. Yes, that man may have set his agenda on her, but she wasn't going to make it easy for him to fulfill it. No matter how much she wanted him to touch her again, to kiss her like he did yesterday, to sweep her off her feet and carry her to his bed and strip off his frayed edged shorts and tight T-shirt, she wasn't going to give up all her control. She wanted a complete relationship this time, not just an empty affair.

Not just an acquaintanceship masquerading as a marriage, she thought with deep sadness. Troubling thoughts, thoughts of a forever kind of love, overwhelmed her when she heard the kitchen phone ringing out its loud command. She raced toward the sound gratefully. She'd even welcome the whispery voiced lady now, anything to fight the confusion that man brought to her heart.

Erin's laughing voice greeted her breathless hello. "Out of breath, girlfriend, I hope I didn't interrupt anything hot and heavy."

Her friend's laughing voice sent her grief back to her unconscious mind. "Nothing like that, Erin, I was only running to get to the phone."

Her laughter warmed Kate's heart, making her realize how much she needed to hear a friendly tone now. "You need to get back to your exercising if that short run left you breathless."

"It wasn't just the run."

"Ooh. And what else could make a woman that out of breath?"

"You're on your honeymoon." A groan sounded through the phone line, a soft sigh of total fulfillment. "So you should already know the answer to that question."

"Man, you can say that again."

"Pretty good?"

"Who would have thought a studious college professor could be so damn good in bed?" Sighs of pleasure rang in Kate's ear, and envy threatened to overwhelm her fragile sexuality. "You won't believe this, Kate, but we actually waited until the wedding night. It was hard but it was worth it."

"Bruce and I waited too." The memory of that time, of how special she'd felt when he'd told her he wanted to wait slipped in with her more confused feelings, enlarging them like a balloon with helium. "I guess things turned out better for you."

"Oh, Kate, I'm sorry I mentioned that. I didn't mean to bring up sad times for you."

Kate forced the useless envy out of her. "Don't let it bother you. Bruce is gone, and I'm trying to remember only the good things about him, and our marriage."

"He was a...decent man."

"Yes, he was generous and kind, faithful and true to the vows of our arrangement." Sadness settled over her, grief burning in the back of her throat. "I just wished he'd wanted me."

"That's still hard for me to believe." Anger laced the alto of her tone. "A trophy wife, you. I still can't believe you actually let him treat you like that."

"He promised to pay so I could finish law school." Kate didn't want to remember this now, the agreement they'd made to keep their farce of a marriage from falling completely apart. "I wanted his money to finish school; he needed me to look sexy and pretty on his arm."

"That must have been so frustrating for you."

Outwardly their marriage looked like a loving, fulfilling match, one that involved hot satisfying nights and loving sweet days. What she'd allowed the world to see was the total opposite of how she'd lived those long five years. Separate beds in separate rooms, long days when she'd keep to her room and he'd kept to his. The only time he'd ever touched her were the rare parties and special occasions when he'd needed to display his trophy on his arm.

"Stop it, Kate," her friend's sharp tone jerked the phone away from her ear, "Stop thinking about that bastard."

"I'm not," she said.

"And stop fibbing about it."

"If only I could understand why I put up with it all those years, I'd be able to let it go." Only Erin remembered the way she'd been before her marriage; only Dana knew what it'd been like during it. No one knew what she was like now, not even her spirit within clamoring to be set free. "If only I understood why I didn't have an affair like most people assumed, like Bruce...wanted me to."

"You didn't because you're a decent woman."

Temper back, she added, "If I was married to that bastard I would've screwed every one of his friends before starting on his enemies. No, I take that back, I'd have started on his enemies." Disgust lingered in her friend's voice.

"I doubt that. You're even more traditional than I am."

"With him," her voice got louder, "I would've changed my ways."

Kate laughed. "I'm so glad you called."

"It's good to hear your voice too."

"So when are you returning to California?" Pushing the lingering memories from her mind, Kate waited for Erin to answer. "I'll be here until the middle of July."

"That's longer, good."

"Good?" A hint of suspicion flicked through her. "What are you up to?"

"Me?" Erin said, "Up to something?"

All her senses went on alert. "When you get all innocent acting, I know you're up to something."

"Believe me; I'm not up to anything." Quick fast breaths belied Erin's words. "I should be back next weekend. I promised to advise my English students on one of the summer stock productions."

"You're hiding something from me."

"No." Erin denied. "I'm…not hiding anything from—anything unreasonable, I mean—from you."

"What?" Erin's jumbled comment made no sense to Kate. "Unreasonable? What do you mean by that?"

"I'm your oldest, dearest friend," Erin whispered, "Am I not?"

"Yes."

"And I'm one of your biggest fans?"

"Yes."

"Don't I know more about your…farce of a marriage than anyone else?"

Not as much as Dana, Kate thought. But Erin

123

understood some of it.

"And I still know you just as well," Erin continued.

"Stop babbling and tell me what you're hiding." Only silence greeted Kate's ears. "Don't you dare go silent on me."

"I only want you to be happy.''

"I'm not unhappy."

Erin's sigh moved through the phone. "I wanted you to meet a...decent guy...who seemed to like you a lot."

"What?"

"Matt."

"What?"

"Don't be mad at me." The voice lowered on the other end, softening in anxiety, before Erin said, "His eyes lit up every time I mentioned your name. I mean, he really lit up. His mom told me he had a crush on you when he was younger, one that he still seemed to have for you. He'd just broken his wedding plans with Anna, and I thought—why the hell not?"

"Oh, Erin," Kate sighed, a weight lifting from her shoulders. "So that's why you decided to elope with your professor the same weekend I planned to come to visit you."

"Are we okay, Kate?"

"Yes."

The rushing laughing sound lifted up Kate's spirits.

"Good, so tell me," Erin whispered, "Do you like him?"

"I like him," came out before Kate could call it back, "I mean, he seems like a nice guy."

"Great! Wonderful!"

Kate could almost feel her friend's infectious smile.

"I knew the two of you would be good together."

Desperate for a change of topic, Kate latched

onto a safer subject. "I met two of those students of yours."

"Oh, you did?" Serious now, Erin asked, "Did they show up at the house? I hope they didn't frighten you."

"I was half asleep, by the pool." Kate hesitated. "They asked where you were but I didn't tell them anything. I didn't know if you wanted anyone to know that you'd gotten married."

"Thanks."

"I also promised them I'd take your place as the show's advisor." She glanced out of the kitchen window, at the silent house near her. "I hope that's all right with you."

"Good," Erin said. "That's what I wanted you to do."

"Yes, I've noticed that," she said easily. "They seem like good kids."

"You've already said that once."

Fate, Kate thought. With the help of her old friend, two old ladies and two young kids, fate was slowly but surely pushing her into a relationship with a certain sexy male.

She wasn't sure if she was ready for this now.

But a part of Kate wanted to try.

****

"Well, that's it." The director placed her clipboard on the table in front of her and swerved to stare at Kate. "Now the fun begins."

Kate grinned at her bemused expression, understanding the reason for it. The lead role had to go to the best performer, and that performer just happened to be Anna. She'd known a few temperamental actors in her time, but how a man like Matthew Hunter could think he loved a woman like that was uncanny. It didn't make any sense at all.

"You probably knew a few people like Anna." Emily's statement broke into Kate's puzzlement, causing her to turn toward the frowning woman. "Maybe you could give me a few pointers. Last year I almost pushed her off the stage a couple of times."

"That might work," Kate said, "It'll teach her some humility."

"You think so?"

"Yes." She leaned into the table. "But only if no one seems to notice."

Emily smiled. "I could arrange that."

They both laughed as they glanced at the complaining woman. Kate breathed in a quick lungful of air at the sight of the thin boy standing all alone near the back of the stage, and a deep aching sense of unfairness invaded her. If there were any justice, that boy would be a much better actor. It hurt to see him so downtrodden.

"It's not right," Kate whispered, "for someone like Anna to have so much talent and a sweet boy like Billy to have...none at all."

"Oh, but the boy does have talent."

"Yes, backstage talent," Kate agreed. "But he should be in the lights, center stage."

Emily smiled at her. "He freezes under those lights."

She nodded, remembering his stilted, mumbling audition.

"And don't sell the boy short. He may not be able to act but when it comes to designing a stage, he's a natural."

"Is he?"

"Almost as good as his dad," Emily said. She stared at Kate for a long time before leaping from the chair and clapping. "Okay, that's enough socializing." She clapped her hands together again, yelling for the crowd to settle down. "Has everyone had a chance to read over their parts?" When affirmative nods and a loud collection of yeses greeted her question, Emily said, "then I guess it's time to do a brief read through of the lines."

"I have a few changes I'll like to suggest."

"There'll be no changes, Anna." The fierce woman stared hard at the actress, and Kate nodded her agreement. "I'm not going to change anything in that script. We'll do it as it was originally written."

"But I...."

"I said no changes."

Kate liked this no-nonsense woman. Maybe they wouldn't have to throw Anna off the stage after all.

The read-through went well except for a few unplanned changes on Anna's part and a few glaring stares on Emily's. Kate felt her soul relaxing in the familiar environment of the spirited first reading. Oh, how she missed this electric atmosphere. The animated voices and wild gestures, mixing with the singers practicing their vocals and the orchestra tuning up in the background, brought all the glimmer and glamour back to her. Maybe she could do the series with Erin. Peacefulness surrounded her; a warm inviting feeling that left her happy and comforted.

"But I want a part this time." The tearful words broke through Kate and she stiffened her back before turning to look behind her. Poor Billy. "Sally gets all the attention."

"Attention she deserves, son."

Matt, she thought in breathless alarm. What is he doing here? Looking through half-closed lids toward the back of the theater, she watched him lower his full head of soft blonde hair closer to the boy's spiked dark ends.

"I should be happy for her, but I'm not," Billy said.

Matt's hand fell onto the boy's shoulder as he whispered words meant for the younger man's ears. Whatever Matt said seemed to work as a full-fledged smile brightened up the boy's sad expression. "Yeah."

"Yes. Your dad told me just last week."

The boy looked across the room toward his father, beaming grin lighting up the area around him. "He liked my ideas for the stage."

"He thinks you're a miracle worker."

Kate jerked her head downward, and stared hard at her fisted hands, when Matt glanced up in her general direction. She tried to act bored at his noisy approach, but his easy, confident stance left her fighting for breath.

"Hi," Matt said.

Thinking he spoke to Emily, she ignored his greeting.

"Kate?"

When she glanced up to where the director had been sitting, she blushed. "Oh."

"The least you can do is say hello."

"I'm sorry." Kate glanced around her, spotting the younger woman on the far side of the theater. *When had Emily moved away from her?* "I thought...."

"Why does it always seem like you want to run away from me?" He spoke the words in jest, but she sensed the seriousness surrounding them. "I thought we'd declared a truce."

"It was only a temporary truce."

"I think we should make it a permanent one." He sat uninvited in Emily's empty chair, so close he brushed her knees with his leg. A rush of heat raced into the lower part of her trembling body as the memory of his kiss filled her. "I like it better when you're laughing and having fun with me."

"I was having fun."

He ignored her declaration. "But now you're frowning and acting like you'd rather be somewhere else. I don't get it. No one here wants to hurt you, Kate."

"I know that." She didn't realize she had acted standoffish and cold toward him. She certainly didn't feel that way now. "I'm sorry if I offended you."

Liquid silver eyes warmed with intense interest. "So could we declare another temporary truce?"

Her lips twisted up at the corners.

"Is that the beginnings of a smile?" He teased. "Yes, I do believe that it is one of your beautiful smiles trying to break through."

"Oh," she said, blushing at his words, "so I'm smiling. It's not the first time you've seen me smile."

"But it's so rare."

Kate knew she must be beaming now. "If you want another temporary truce, you're going to have to tell me what you just said to Billy. He looked so depressed until you whispered to him."

Matt grinned. "That's between me and the boy."

"You're not going to tell me." She placed her hand on his firm thigh, and quickly pulled it away. "Well, that's your right. I'm just glad he's feeling better."

"Why did you do that?" His glance focused on her fisted hands. "I like you touching me."

"It's…not proper."

"Why?" Before he could ask another question, a set of camera flashes brightened the area around her. "What? Where did she come from?" Matt turned to the reporter. "Kate doesn't want her picture taken now."

"Katherine, could I ask you a couple of questions?" The photographer pointed her tape recorder in her face. "Are you going—?"

"Her name is Kate," Matt said, blocking the insistent reporter from her. "I don't think she wants to answer any of your questions."

"Matt, I'm fine."

"You don't need to—"

"Katherine, I heard through the rumor mill that you're thinking of doing the television pilot show of 'Three Sisters' with Erin Fitzgerald. Is that true?"

"It's a rumor," Matt said.

"Matt," silencing him with a soft touch, Kate

129

turned to the reporter. "I have been offered the part, but I haven't decided yet if I'm going to take it."

"I heard the other two principle actresses have already agreed to do the series," pressing the recorder to her face, "And that you're the lone hold-out. Why? Are you asking for more money?"

Surprised Kate stared over at Matt for a moment. Ignoring the second part of the reporter's statement, she said, "I believe one of them has given an affirmative answer. Erin and I are still in the discussion stage. In fact, I'm here to speak with my friend about the series."

"Rumor has it that Ms. Fitzgerald signed the contract a few weeks ago."

Erin already signed the contract? Kate thought. No, she wouldn't have hidden that fact from her.

"Well," Matt stepped in front of her. "You shouldn't believe everything you hear."

"My sources are top notch, Ms. Adams." Ignoring Matt, the reporter looked at her. "They are sources whom I trust to give me the truth."

"My name is Mrs. Williams." Fury burned hot in her gut, sending her temper to the surface. "Kate Williams."

"I'm sorry, but—"

"You need to back off now." Matt pulled her out of her chair, pulling her into his arms. Kate wrapped her arms around his waist. "She has nothing more to say to you."

As they walked toward the raised stage area, the reporter flung out one more question. Stunned people stood quiet around the room, taking it all in with differing expression. "If Erin didn't agree to do the series, why did its director make the announcement in today's paper saying she did?"

Kate froze on the top step.

"You can read the article yourself."

She moved her head from Matt's chest and turned to the grinning woman. "I don't believe you."

"I'll leave the paper—opened to the entertainment page." The reporter placed the paper on the table. "You can believe it or not, but it won't make this article any less true."

As a final parting shot, she lifted up her camera and took another set of pictures.

"Are you all right?" Matt asked, a second after the door closed on the reporter. "Kate?"

"Yes, yes." Kate slipped from his loosening embrace, but didn't move away from him. "Do you think she was telling the truth?"

"There's only one way to find out." He took her hand and led her to the table. "Read it."

After reading the short piece, she handed it to the man beside her and sank into her empty chair. It was true, Kate thought. Erin did sign the contract to do the series. She didn't look up at him as she stared out at the empty theater. Where had all the others gone? When did they all leave her? And who told that reporter she was working here in the first place? No one knew she'd decided to help out at the summer stock theater.

"You didn't tell me she'd decided to do the series." Matt said.

His accusation hurt her more than all the others in her past, and there had been so many other times. "I didn't know."

He stared at her, emptiness blacking out all light from his expressive eyes.

"Matt, don't look at me like that."

"How am I supposed to look at you, Kate?" Dry bitterness sang in his voice. "I was beginning to trust you."

"Matt?"

"I was starting to believe you were telling me the truth."

"Matt!"

His tone lowered in despair. "What a fool I've been."

"I...didn't know about Erin." When they innocently touched this time, Matt was the one to jerk away. "I don't understand why you won't believe me. Why do you always want to believe the worst of me?"

His broad back moved away from her, and she sensed her answer.

****

"What is wrong with you?"

"Mom, why are you calling so early?" Stretching his arms toward the nightstand, Matt grabbed the clock and stared at the large numbers. "Don't you realize it's five in the morning?"

"I'm aware of the time." His mother's temper leaped through the phone line, forcing him to straighten up in the bed. "How could you accuse her of doing such a thing?"

Swinging his legs over the edge of the bed, Matt pressed his heels into the rough tan carpet. "Mom, it's way too early for such a complicated question."

"Complicated?"

"I need...coffee."

"You need—" He heard her swallowing hard, breathing in and out a few loud gasps before she said, "I talked to Kate last night. She hid her hurt well, but I knew she'd been crying."

This brought him up out of his seat. "Kate was crying. Why was she crying?"

"You should know the answer to that."

He feared he did. "Oh, Mom."

"Don't oh, mom me, Matt." He heard hot anger leap from her words. "I don't understand you at all anymore. When she told me about that newspaper article, I knew she was being truthful. I knew she didn't know Erin had already signed that contract."

"Mom?"

"Why do you always think she's lying to you?"

He jumped up from the bed, knocking the phone half off the stand before pushing it back against the wall.

"Matt?"

Why *did* he always think the worst of her? Because she was an actress like Anna, because she needed a backer for her comeback television series like Anna needed a backer for her movie, because she wasn't like the woman he'd been infatuated with at the tender age of fifteen?

Didn't Kate's decreased husband leave her well off? Anna needed him to back her big break, but Kate could finance her come-back show with her own money. She didn't need his millions, did she?

Dear Lord, could he be *that* shallow?

"Matt, are you all right?"

Could he be upset because she wasn't coming on to him like he'd always imagined she would do if they'd ever met, because she didn't act like that sexy character she'd portrayed over ten years ago, because she wasn't 'Monica'? Was he upset because she wasn't still *the* Katherine Adams?

"Don't you dare ignore me, Matthew Hunter."

"Mom."

"Where did you go?" Concern sounded in her voice. "I thought you'd fallen or something."

"I think I know why I've been getting so angry about that series," whispered Matt. "It's not about the money at all."

"What are you talking about now?"

He breathed deep from his lungs. "I've carried an image of Kate for years with me, and the reality...of her doesn't fit that image."

"Why would you think it should?"

Ignoring her, he added, "I thought I'd gotten over my infatuation with Katherine Adams years ago, I guess a part of me still held on to that infatuation."

Silence whispered through the phone. "You'll hurt her."

"I don't want to hurt her." His decision made, he

stood tall and firm next to the bed. Power and strength flowed into him as his decision solidified in his mind. If he wanted to get beyond his teen feelings for the woman, he had to fulfill them. "I want to be...." He stopped his statement before he said more than he wanted his mother to know.

"Kate's the same person as Katherine. If you make love to her, you need to be aware of that."

His mother understood more than he gave her credit for. "I need to get the past out of my system before I can move into the future."

Confusion filled the air, in his mom's voice, in his own mind. 'She's not that young, sexy actress anymore, Matt."

"She is to me."

"Matt, you're wrong about her."

He realized that, yet—he wanted that young, sexy actress. "Why did you call me so early?"

"She's not—"

"You said she was upset."

"Close to tears," whispered his mother, giving up on the more intense conversation. "I called to tell you how mad I was at you, and to tell you to go tell her you're sorry for making her cry. But now I'm not so sure that's a good idea."

"Why?"

Silence greeted his one word before she said, "Her past is still with her." His mother hung up the phone after saying this cryptic comment. He wanted to slam his own down hard, to release some of the pain of his shallowness, but he didn't.

Exhaling and weaving his fingers through his messed hair, he headed to the bathroom. A knock sounded on the hotel room door a few second after he'd finished with his morning routine. He pulled on a pair of jean shorts and walked to the door, expecting to see his partner. Today was a big day for both of them; today he planned to start the final move into his new headquarters.

But Carlos didn't enter the room at his greeting. Instead a whirlwind of flowery scents and flowing, dark brown hair blew into the room and stopped in front of him. A spray of angry words yelled from her tight mouth as tiny hands pounded against his naked chest.

It stung him. "Mary?"

"You are a fool," she cried. "A complete fool."

"What did I do now?" Lifting up his spread fingers toward the furious woman, he glanced behind her at her smirking husband. "Carlos, get this woman of yours off of me."

"You're on you own, man."

"What did I do?"

"Your guess is as good as mine," Carlos said.

Her fingers pointed into Matt's face. "You will not hurt that woman."

Kate, he thought.

"You will not use her like you used all the others." Mary's tone quieted as she dropped her clenched fists from his bare chest and stepped back into her husband's encircling arms, exhausted from the pounding she'd inflicted on him. He had a feeling he deserved the beating. "Kate deserves better than that."

"What?" Matt's gaze sprang once again to the smirking Carlos. "My mom called you?"

"Your mom called her." Nodding down toward his wife's flushed face, he added, "I guess your mom was pretty upset. What's going on anyway?"

Another set of biting words rose from deep in the woman's throat, in Spanish this time. The tone of her voice, the spark burning in her eyes, left no doubt as to the meaning of the words. Even if he didn't understand the language, he understood the nonverbal animation in her features with total clarity.

"Nothing's going on Carlos." He moved away from the cradling couple and reached for a shirt he'd lain out on the chair the night before and covered his upper body. "Now if you don't mind, I'll like to finish getting dressed."

"Where do you plan on going?" Mary's haughty voice stirred an aching need deep from his memories, bringing his decision even closer to the surface. "If you hurt Kate, I swear I'll come back here and hurt you."

He turned and looked hard at her, softening his attitude toward her at the look in Carlos' eyes. Kate had found a firm friend in this fierce, protective woman, and in his mother, he thought. "Look, I need to settle feelings from my past before I can figure out what to do with my future."

"And how will you do that?" Mary asked.

"I'll know when it happens."

****

He knew what he wanted to do.

Matt swallowed in a deep cleansing breath and placed his fisted hand against the door, freezing his movement when he heard a soft sigh filtering through the living room. Want jerked into him, as he remembered other sighs issuing from this same woman when she'd played all those sexy characters, in those movies he'd watched over and over during his fifteenth year. A sigh of need sounded clear in her throat just before the man who'd played her lover in that one movie kissed her. It had set his heart on fire, rushing blood from his brain to his youthful penis. The same sound, the same sigh he'd just heard coming from the quietness of the house, stopped his heart and engorged his middle with hot blood, sending an aching rush of desire through his hardening body.

No, he couldn't do this to the woman. He wanted her but not like this. Giving the door a light touch, he turned around and strode to the car he'd left parked on the street.

He didn't know what to do about his feelings.

Matt sat for a long time outside the home where the woman of his youthful infatuation lived, his mother's neighbor. What should he do? He should go up to the door again and tell her how sorry he was for acting the way he did at the rehearsal, for believing that reporter and not letting her talk. He wasn't sure he could do that without pushing his way into her home, without pushing her into something they both might regret.

He wanted her, yet he wanted it to be a mutual thing.

Slamming his hand against the steering wheel of his car, he glanced over at his mother's front window and sighed. The curtain moved to the side as he watched and he saw the beautiful features of his tiny parent.

Was his mother right? Would Mary be right if he made love to Kate now?

Yes, he would hurt her. He glanced once more at her house before turning on his ignition and driving away. He could wait until the Chamber of Commerce dinner.

Chapter Eleven

Sweet seduction, Kate thought hanging up the phone a few seconds after the whispery-voiced woman disconnected the call. The warning lingered in her ears as she sank down in the kitchen chair. Seduction only for the sake of getting her into his bed, of getting what he wanted from her before telling her good-bye, the caller had implied.

And he'd done it to Erin, used her and thrown her away. At least that's what the woman had told her. But did she believe it?

"No." Slamming her hand against the table, Kate laid her head into her folded arms and fought back the slow burn of tears. "No."

The front door chimed as she wiped the last of her tears away. She ignored it and sank her head back to her arms, allowing the years of pent-up emotions to wash her heart clean.

"Kate?"

"Are you there?"

Two distinct voices called out her name almost at the same time from the direction of the back door. A hard, loud knock accompanied the anxious words.

"Girl, we see you at the table." Grace's gruff tone showed her concern. "What's wrong with you? Open the door. Now!"

"Grace, calm down."

"What did that boy of yours do to her this time?"

Anger bit in the other woman's voice. "And why do you assume Matt did anything to her? I know he said....Oh, Grace."

"Just look at her, Esther."

Kate glanced up toward the door, spying the outline of the two women in the frilly white half-curtains.

"He just left her a little bit ago," Grace continued, "And now she's sitting at the table howling her little eyes out."

"Yes, she does seem to be crying."

Kate lifted from her chair and grabbed a flowered paper towel from the roll hanging nearby. Unlocking the door, she turned and sat back down in her chair, the unused paper towel still whole between her trembling fingers. A hard hand clamped around her shoulder, a softer one laid on the other while the two women flanked her. Kate wiped her face dry.

"Ready to talk now, girl?" The bigger lady let go of her shoulder to heave her bulk into the nearest chair. "What did that boy do to you?"

"I'm all right, Grace."

"Sure, we all cry when everything is going fine and dandy."

Esther's soft fingers moved from her shoulders to linger on her drying cheek for only a second before she sat down into a chair opposite her.

"Don't let Grace upset you, dear."

"She hasn't upset me."

"That damn son of yours has already done the damage." Jerking her eyes from the smaller woman to Kate, Grace asked, "So what did Matt want just now?"

"I haven't seen him since the practice."

"Oh, quit your fibbing," Grace said loudly, "We just watched him leave this house, get in his car, and drive away."

"He wasn't here." Surprise sounded in her voice, even to her own ears. Why was Matt standing by her door? Why didn't he knock and come in? "He didn't do anything."

"I told you to quit fibbing."

"Grace." Calmness settled into the larger woman's demeanor as she stared at her smaller friend, stillness that filled Kate's being as well. Had he come to tell her he was sorry for how he'd acted earlier?

"Now tell us why you're so upset. If my son didn't just visit with you, why are you so upset? If my son did anything to hurt you, I swear I'll talk to him about it. The both of us will."

"I got a phone call from the same person who called and told me you were in danger."

"That rotten little boy," said Grace. "Is that why you're crying now?"

"It wasn't a little boy." She glanced from the larger woman to the smaller one. "Did Erin and Matt ever...get together?"

"Ever what, dear?" Esther asked. "Are you asking us if your friend and my son ever slept together?"

"My caller seemed to think they did." Tears threatened to overwhelm her again, but she forced them back behind her tight eyelids. "She implied he used her, and that I'll be a fool if I allowed him close to me."

Grace slammed her hand against the table. "Why the little witch! Everyone knows Erin's in love with Jack."

"She's in the Caribbean, on her honeymoon." Joy filed past the emptier feelings at Grace's statement, drying all the unshed tears from her heart. "No, I should've realized she wouldn't do that. She wouldn't sleep with one man when she was in love with another."

"What are you muttering about now?" Grace asked.

Taking a deep breath, Kate sat straight in her chair and stared at the smaller woman. "But I need to hear it from you, Esther. Did Matt and Erin make love?"

"So that's what you've been worrying about." Grace hit her fist so hard against the edge of the chair it leaped its hind legs off the floor. "You think Matt and Erin made love?"

"The strange phone calls I've been getting lately," Kate said lightly, "tell me they did."

"His mother probably won't admit this, but we did try to get them together."

Kate stared at the two older women as they exchanged one of those slightly suspicious looks, spying a slight guilt shining in their eyes. Why the guilt now? What have they been up to now?

Grace continued, "Neither one seemed interested."

"Your friend had her eyes on that professor friend of hers from the college." Esther's calm tone once again quieted Kate's feelings. "Matt and Erin became friends, only friends."

"Friends?"

"Of course, dear." The older woman's fingers lay softer on her stilled arm. "You just said she wouldn't do that."

"She wouldn't but—"

"No buts, girl." Grace's large hand pressed to the side of her face. "Now tell us about that phone caller."

"Like I said, it seemed to be the same person who told me Esther was in trouble. But I'm not sure if it was. That call seemed different from the most recent ones somehow." Kate stood and walked to the sink. Cold running water washed over her wrist and hands a few seconds later. "I just hung up the phone after her last call only a few minutes ago. I don't know why she wants to confuse me about Matt."

"Are you sure it's a woman?" Grace said while looking quickly at her friend.

"I wasn't sure at first, but now...yes." She stared at the larger woman. "I recognized that voice though. I know I've heard it before, somewhere."

141

"Dear, maybe you should call the police."

"That wouldn't do any good."

"Why not," Esther asked. "You're being threatened, aren't you?"

She bit at her lower lip and glared at the stream of cold water.

"Kate?"

Glancing at the quiet smaller woman, she shook her head slowly.

"Are your thoughts settled about Erin and Matt?" When she didn't answer her after a long moment, Esther sounded puzzled. "You must believe me; Matt never touched your friend. I don't believe he's been with a woman in six or seven months."

"And he's better off without Anna."

Kate didn't really want to know but something deep inside her made her ask the question anyway. "Why is that?"

"That little witch only wanted his money, is all."

"He accused me of the same thing." She turned off the hard running water before turning towards the two frowning women. "I don't have any need for his money. I know somehow my office sent him a copy of the script for the series, but I didn't authorize it. I came here with the intention of discussing the series with Erin. I really didn't know she'd already decided to do the show."

"We believe you, girl." Grace's hard gaze lifted from her face to fall onto her friends. "We're mad at Matt."

"I'm glad you told me." She squeezed Esther's tiny fingers, and smiled. "I know you're right."

"Maybe Matt can look after you too." Esther stared into her face. "Yes, I think Matt should be your bodyguard."

"I don't think I'm in any danger." She liked the thought of being near him. But still—"Maybe you might be."

"Why, did she tell you I was in danger, dear?"

Tightening her hold on her fingers, the small woman reached up with her other hand to caress a soft finger over her smooth cheek. The gesture reminded her of Matt, yet the effects were totally different. No jumping heartbeat and drying mouths, only soft concern and caring lingered in her touch. "I don't think you should bother with her. She must have something on my son."

"But why me?" she asked. "If this person has something against Matt, why would she target me? If I were trying to get back at someone, I'd use the persons' weaknesses. And his weaknesses should be the two of you."

"You would think so."

The look that passed between the two older women left Kate even more bewildered than the strange phone calls. *What are the two of you up to?* Why did they seem so sure she was the woman's real target?

But still it did help her realize how wrong she'd been for believing the rumors about Erin. Erin would never allow a man to use and abuse her the way the caller implied Matt had done. No, Erin was always so sure of her own worth, her own sexuality, and if her friend had already given her heart to another, nothing would get in her way. No matter how forceful, how handsome and sexy, no matter how rich, Erin would never be tempted by another man. She would've lost too much to gain only a one-night stand.

No, Erin never slept with Matt.

So why did that woman want her to believe she had?

****

"It's quiet out there today." Carlos sank into one of the plush chairs in front of Matt's revamped corner office, stretching his long legs out in front of him. "I didn't see any of the usual construction workers hanging around the place."

"That's because they're finished with the remodeling." Matt stretched out his own legs, filling up the room with his linebacker-like shoulders and six foot four inches of pure bulk. "I walked through the building with the foreman this morning, and I liked what I saw."

"I'm surprised they're done already." Carlos looked around him before reaching down to the floor and placing his ever present notebook on the mahogany desk. "I thought it would take a few weeks to get all the renovations you wanted done."

"They did a good job."

"Yes." Glancing around the room again, the man nodded before lifting up its top and booting up the notebook's system. "That's good, man; because I just found out we have another problem to worry about."

Matt turned to watch his partner type on the keypad. "We got another problem?"

"Yes, afraid so," Carlos said absentmindedly while typing in a few more words. "Do you have any reason why a law firm in Seattle is asking to search our records?" Not waiting for an answer, he tapped a few more keys and turned the machine to face him. "I saved this application from a firm called Williams, Williams, Gay, & Brown."

"Williams, Williams, Gay, & Brown?"

"You know them?"

"Kate's from—" Grabbing the machine from his friend's hand, he swore softly under his breath. "I can't believe she would do this!"

"You do know what this is about!"

"It's an application to check out last years' financial reports in regard to a certain television series deal."

"A television deal?" Carlos' confusion sang loud in the room. "I thought we've already decided against backing Erin's series."

"TopNotch did."

"Then why the new check?"

144

"Katherine Adams."

"Oh. Kate." Carlos frowned. "I thought the two of you've been getting along. Didn't you take her out to dinner the other night?"

Matt frowned toward his friend before turning his glance back to the drab wall. The gray linen of his suit pants and black of his shoes stood out in stark contrast against the darkness of the large room.

"You don't still believe she's only here to get you to finance that series, do you?"

"Yes, I do," Matt said.

"Do your mom and aunt know about this?"

Carlos knew the ladies' way too well, Matt thought.

"Or are they acting all innocent and sweet?"

"Sometimes I feel like...."

"Yeah, I can understand that. If my parents and other assorted family members were like your mother and aunt, I would never get any rest." He smiled his trademark sideways grin. "But I would be one very happy, satisfied man."

"It's a good thing you weren't an only child," Matt added, "and you're happily married."

"Yeah." Carlos laughed. "At times like this, I'm glad I have all those brothers and sisters."

When Matt didn't comment on his statement, the Hispanic man asked, "So has our sexy ex-actress played her best hand yet?"

"Almost."

"Oh, man." His interest shined clear in his dark eyes as he leaned into the desk to get a better view of Matt's face. "Don't leave this old married guy in distress. Talk."

"Kate's...different."

"Not as sexy and sultry as all her characters?" His wicked grin sent a rush of unexpected anger into his center. "Don't tell me she's gotten all pure and innocent on you?"

"No, she's still as sexy as ever." Moaning around his raised hands, he remembered that afternoon, sitting outside of Erin's house. He wanted to go inside, needed to get Katherine Adams out of his system, but he couldn't do it. He couldn't hurt the woman she had become. "Kate Williams is so much more sensual than Katherine Adams."

"She's only one person, Matt." Carlos reached over to slap at his arm. "They're one and the same."

"Fifteen years removed and a not so happy marriage apart." Suddenly lifting from his memories, Matt stared at his friend. "Two can play at this game."

"What are you up to now?"

Matt watched his eyes register a slight wariness, sensing his friend's discomfort. But he didn't care.

"I don't like what I'm reading in your face," Carlos added.

"She's attempting to check up on TopNotch; it's only fair that I check up on Williams, Williams, Gay, & Brown."

"For what purpose?"

"Kate's husband," he answered.

"Isn't your lady's husband dead?"

"Yes," came out, before the accusation in his friend's voice sank in. "And Kate is *not* my lady."

"If she isn't your lady," the man stared a truthful look at him, "why haven't you already taken her to bed? I know you've had countless opportunities."

"Kate's different."

"Kate's more than just a quick lay for you, Matt." Reaching over the desk, the balding man clamped his fingers around his wide shoulder. "You may not know it yet but this Kate Williams has touched your heart."

"Oh, don't bet on that."

"I see it in your eyes every time you say her

name." Matt watched his smile deepen. "The look I
see now in your eyes is the same look I had in my
own when I met Mary."

"Oh, don't be ridiculous."

"Mark my words, you've got it bad for this
woman."

"Be real, Carlos." Matt lifted his weight out of
the desk chair and stretched his arms over his head
in a long relaxing way. "I'll admit I wouldn't mind
taking her to bed but that's it. No commitment, no
complications."

"Then why haven't you've been with her?"

"It's…." He almost said complicated. "It's not the
right time. I have too much going on right now, and
I'm still not interested in being a part of a deal like
the one she's after. I'm still not sure of the reason
she's here."

"Have you even read the script?"

"No."

"Why not?"

"It's—"

"Yeah, I know," he leaned toward him, "It's
complicated."

Chapter Twelve

When Matt arrived at Erin's front door at exactly fifteen to six that balmy Saturday night, dressed in a tight-fitting black tuxedo with a silk white shirt and gray cummerbund, Kate sensed trouble. It seemed to sing out of his silvery-gray eyes and straight overpowering stance as she opened the door and stepped back for him to enter the front room. For once, a sharp vulnerability weakened her body, making it hard to breathe. She'd promised to be his 'trophy' date, to look sexy and demure, sultry and willing on his arms. Yet, this time being a trophy woman troubled her more than the many times she'd played the same role for her husband. Here, with this man, she wanted it to end in a different way. She wanted this night to end in his bed with the sexy red and white dress in a heap on the floor and her under his body, moaning out his name.

Oh, she was a mess.

"You're lovely."

"Thank you." Her need didn't sound in her voice, didn't reveal itself in the flirty glance. "You look good yourself."

He smiled. "I'm going to be the envy of the party."

"No, I will be." Feeling slightly more at ease, she decided to enjoy the evening. She did feel beautiful tonight. The brand-new dress set her back a few hundred dollars, as well as the new bouncier hairstyle and manicure; this date had cost her more than her last three dates in Seattle.

"I don't think I want to share you."

His words sang clear in her soul. "And why is that?"

Reaching for her hand, he twirled her around a few times in front of him before jerking her bare back into his front. A rush of heat moved into her lower body at his sudden embrace. "I want to press my kiss on those creamy breasts of yours while caressing my hand down your soft back."

Breathless she leaned her head against his chest. The scent of something woodsy issued from his body as she closed her eyes. "I think I want that too." Turning into his arms, she reached her hands up to trace the rugged skin of his face with one long finger. He stiffened tight at her demanding touch, pulling back from her. "What's wrong?"

"We need to be on our way." Rejection slid in to her heart, cooling the desire burning deep in her. "Do you have a wrap?"

"No."

He glanced over her slowly, almost in a sensual way, before he moved his hot eyes from her and spied a soft white shawl near the door. "You better put this on otherwise you might get cold."

Why? She wanted to ask, but she only turned her back and accepted the soft material around her shoulders. It did fit her well, and it did cover the low material barely covering her pronounced bosom and back. Why had she wasted her money on such a revealing dress anyway? What was she thinking?

"Are you ready to go?"

Matt's smile confused her. Hot and cold; touching and caring one minute, standoffish the next, the man left her feeling more bewildered by the second.

Well, two can play at his type of game.

Twirling only her blonde head in his direction, she allowed the smooth shawl to slide slowly down her right arm. Slight desire flared in his mild gray eyes, burning a blaze of fire into her right side. The rejection she'd been experiencing lifted from her mind.

"You like this dress?" Flirting with the man felt better than fighting. "I can tell you like it."

"Oh, Katie, you're the most beautiful woman I've seen in a long time."

"Katie, I like it." Smiling she pulled the white shawl up over her shoulders. "No one ever calls me Katie."

"From Katherine Adams to Kate Williams," he teased, "Katie doesn't quite fit the image."

"I like Katie."

"But not Katherine," he asked. "You don't like anyone calling you Katherine."

She pulled the wrap tighter around her shoulders. "My name is Kate now."

"You're one and the same person."

"You would think," she mumbled. "I'm all ready to go."

"What's wrong?"

"I'm just hungry." Ignoring his questioning look, she swerved a studied provocative glance his way, while allowing the shawl to drop lower on her back this time. "And I'm ready to play my part."

Anger darkened the black of his eyes for a brief moment while his stance straightened in a rigid line. An excited breath, a lost heartbeat later, he relaxed and grinned wicked at her. His look said if you want to play a part then you'd better play it well.

Oh, what did she think she was doing? Playing with this formidable man would only hurt her.

"Come on."

Stepping ahead of him while he held the door open, she stopped at his BMW. His hand brushed against the side of her neck when he reached past her to open the passenger side door. Kate settled into the comfortable seat and waited in silence as he closed the door and walked around the car to his side.

He stopped halfway into his seat and waved in the general direction of his aunt's house. "We've got an audience."

Kate grinned. "When don't we?"

Dark eyes caressed over her delicately made-up face. "If they want their plan to succeed, they'll have to leave us in peace."

Kate's sudden laughter startled his look back to her, startled her own bemused feelings. A frown played over the edges of his mouth. "I was thinking about my brothers."

He grinned then before turning back to the road. After driving out of the housing complex he finally said, "I guess they never let you have any alone time."

"I learned to be a very good—" Glancing quickly up toward him she decided finishing this sentence would only upset the balance of their relationship now, she froze the words in her lungs. "If I wanted to go out on a date, or even spend a night with my girlfriends, I had to get my mom to tell them to back off."

"You should've told them to leave you be."

"Sure, and *that* would've worked." Sarcasm laced loud in her voice. "To this day my oldest brother still threatens men I bring home."

"Have there been many?"

His tone confused her. "No, not for a while now." Something like jealousy, a hint of want shined deep in his beautiful silvery eyes. "I've only dated a few men since my husband's death. It's easier that way."

"It may be," he whispered, "but it sounds lonely."

"Yes." Peering up at him through half-closed lids, she lowered her voice. "But you've been alone lately, according to your mom and aunt, and Emily. I should be honored."

"Yeah, you should." The want in his eyes

deepened, causing her to swallow hard at its implication. "You're the first woman I've felt comfortable with in a long while."

His soft answer stunned her with its honesty. Yet something in his voice held back the total truth. He wanted her to believe his words—and she did believe them—but she wasn't too sure if they were the whole truth.

This was not the same man who'd left her hot and aching a week ago.

Silence lingered in the quiet car the rest of the short trip to the large party hall ten miles outside of town. Kate stared up in awe at the modern facility with flowing lines, a well-maintained garden blocking her view of the large front entrance. As Matt helped her out of the car and handed the keys to the young man near him, she grinned up at the imposing structure.

"Are you ready to go inside?"

She only nodded, speechless as she walked ahead of him towards the sounds of laughter.

They were greeted by a middle-aged man with an obvious hairpiece. "Good to see you, Mr. Hunter."

"It's an honor to be here, Mayor." Placing his hands on the small of her back, he pulled her nearer to his side. "And Mrs. Simmons, you look nice tonight."

"Why, thank you."

The mayor wife's sharp eyes fell upon Kate as she patted her upswept hairstyle with a brightly manicured hand. She stepped nearer to her husband when she turned to look at her. "And who is this lovely creature?"

Kate wanted to scream.

"This is Kate Williams." Matt's hand encircled her waist now, twirling tiny heat producing swirls of burning fire into her side. "She's a friend of Erin Fitzgerald."

"Yes, Erin and I have known each other for

years."

"You're an actress too," the mayor said, "I think I remember you."

"I thought you looked familiar." The thin aging woman grabbed her husband's arm and pulled him away. "It's nice to meet you. Come on dear, we need to mingle with all the guests. We must not be rude."

"Dear, I need to talk with Matt for a few minutes."

"It can wait until Monday." The haughty older woman pulled the man away from them. "It's good to meet you, Mr. Hunter."

Kate sighed.

"Couldn't get him away from you quick enough, could she?" He turned her into him, not releasing the hold on her waist or stopping the small sexy movements of his fingers against her bare skin. She liked this nearness between, liked the awareness lingering in his sensual caress. His touch made the older woman's attitude easier to bear. "Doesn't it get to you? I mean, having women shun you like that?"

"I'm used to it."

"But still..." Placing his thumb under her chin, he smiled into her eyes. "You're with me tonight. Why would she even need to worry about you and her husband?"

"Because he's the mayor," she said simply.

"Yes, he is." He pulled her closer to his front and she sighed as he slid his hands from her back to cup her bottom. "But I'm much better looking."

She laughed. "But you're still not the mayor."

"But I do own a lucrative security business, and I am worth a couple of million dollars. Doesn't that count for something? And I have my own hair." He leaned closer to her. She trembled as his warm breath breezed into the shell of her ear. "And no woman has ever left me unsatisfied."

Shock raced through her system at the implication of his statement. "Matt?"

"I doubt the mayor can say the same."

"You're wicked."

"Did I shock you, Katie?" He pressed his front hard into her, wrapping his arms around her and pulling her onto the dance floor. "Just wait until you feel me naked."

His whispered words heated her skin, causing the ache in her middle to soften and swirl to her weak legs. An urgent need like she'd never experienced before with any other man raced through her. "Matt, you need to calm down."

Kate liked this feeling.

"Did I shock you?" He twirled her around the floor. "Tell me."

"Yes."

"Good." He pulled her tighter in his arms and danced her to the edge of the room, stopping in a secluded little alcove between an empty table and a large potted plant. Hot pulsating need rushed through her body as he gazed with intense eyes at her while lifting her chin to cup it in his firm grasp. "I know I promised to go slow with you. But, Katie, I ache for you."

"Matt."

He nibbled her earlobe and before she knew it her arms snaked around his middle, hands playing over the rough material of his back in rhythm with the slow music. She wanted this man with a passion like she'd never known, ached for him to satisfy her need.

"Tonight, Katie."

His promise melted the bones of her legs, making them feel rubbery and weak under her. "Don't you dare let me go."

"Don't worry." Twisting her sideways a few inches, she groaned as the hard length of his middle pressed into her aching stomach. "I'm afraid my reaction to your nearness is way too obvious right now."

"Nice," she said

A groan roughened his arrogant reply. "Nice is not the word I was looking for, I don't feel very nice."

"Oh, you poor baby." Her voice deepened in a sultry way. She lowered her lips over the edge of his grin, kissing his mouth softly. "It seems like you're going to need some help taking care of that little problem."

He only groaned again before crushing her hand into his tight body and twirling her around the dance floor. And for a change she didn't mind that he'd reacted to her 'Monica' voice. Because somehow, she knew deep inside he thought of Kate Williams when he heard that sexy voice, and not Katherine Adams.

She was Katherine and Kate, Monica and all the other sensual characters she'd ever played. Now, she was beginning to understand what everyone had always told her. They were—all of them—a part of her.

After Matt finally loosened his embrace and led her to a table where Carlos sat with his pretty wife, the night seemed to drag. Even though Matt's friends and business associates spoke almost non-stop about his endless supply of relatives, with Mary adding a few telling remarks here and there during a lull in the conversation, Kate found her eyes drifting to the smiling man sitting close to her. If Carlos had asked her what he'd just said that made everyone laugh, she would have been hard pressed to remember. Yes, a part of her laughed when the others laughed, smiled when the others at the table smiled. Yet she didn't remember any of his actual words.

All she could remember of the party was the way Matt's glance seemed to settle on her face at the oddest moments, the way she felt tight in his arms when they danced, the way she barely heard the compliments and noticed the adoring looks from the other party-goers.

And on her way home with him a few hours later, Kate burned with an aching knowledge that this homecoming would end up different. The drive seemed to last for hours until she finally recognized the entrance to her friend's housing complex. She started to open the car before Matt stopped her movement with a rough touch and a blunt shake of his head. Anticipation sang deep in her body, settling hot in her center.

"Damn." Pulling her from the car, he trapped her against the open door. He felt so alive and restless next to her. "Our little peepers are standing by my aunt's front door."

"They won't come over here." Sneaking a look at the two, she sighed. "Would they?"

"Kiss me, Kate."

She almost laughed at the words, but her need for laughter died as another more powerful emotion filled her. His kiss devoured her, catching her unaware as her exhaled breath mixed with his inside the space of his mouth. Suddenly his lips moved from hers, lingering near her parted mouth as he stared past her flushed face. "They're gone."

"Why do I somehow doubt that?"

He moved his lips close to her ear. "My Mom *is* looking out the window."

"I figured," she whispered back. "So are they going to get their wish?"

Instead of saying a word, he only grabbed her hand and pulled her away from the car door. He held tight to her hand as he slammed the door hard and locked the vehicle, never taking his eyes off of her. His gaze moved over her, studying her within the dim light of the nearby streetlights.

"What's your wish, Katie?" Something disquieting raced through his eyes as he asked this question, doubt mixed with distrust. "Do you want me?"

"Yes, I want you."

He moaned out her name and jerked her up against him. Her fingers trembled as she attempted to unlock the front door. Soon it opened freely and she walked into the cool living room first. She stood silent and still as he closed and locked the door behind them, afraid to move, afraid to speak. Yet, when the white garment started to fall from her bare shoulders, Kate shrugged low to help it drop to the floor.

"Katie?"

"I like it when you call me that." Turning to him, she dragged in a long breath before stepping into his wide embrace. "Only you call me that."

"Good." Pushing her away, he pulled his jacket off in a slow, timed way before undoing the black tie and cummerbund, and unbuttoning the white shirt. "And only I will ever call you that."

"I'd like that."

A secret little smile played around his softening mouth as he muttered something she didn't quite hear. The sight of his bare, tanned chest trapped her breath low in her lungs, slammed the beat of her heart hard against the walls of her chest. Her breasts tightened at the sight of his naked body coming to full view as he slowly shed one piece of clothing after another until even his black boxers lay on the floor by his bare feet.

"You still think I'm only nice."

Kate could barely breathe as the sight of him filled her senses with a fiery desire so strong it hurt her. *Tear my brand-new three hundred dollar dress to shreds and throw me against the wall,* she wanted to tell him. But only a single moan moved out of her clenched lungs.

It was enough.

"Come here."

Suddenly shy, she stood frozen.

"Katie, I want you."

Moving into his trembling arms, she sank her lips to his wide chest and kissed him gently an inch from the hardened bud of his nipple. He groaned loud when she flicked her tongue gently over it, unusual shyness gone. He dragged in a loud uneven gasp but stood still as she moved out of his loose embrace and stared at his shaking body. Where her look touched, she placed her anxious hand and explored the contours of his expansive chest, the hard length of his muscled arms, up to the hard coil of his tight neck and shoulders. He moaned again when she moved into him, encircling her arms around to feel the smooth surface of his back. The evidence of his need pressed hot into her clothed front, causing her stomach to cramp with desperation and urgent desire.

As if reading her mind, he stepped behind her and unzipped the short metal enclosure slowly down the curve of her bottom, placing his hands on her waist to push the material away. She shivered, stepping without help out of the expensive dress as it landed on the floor around her sandaled feet. Kicking off her shoes Kate sighed and swerved toward him with a gentle touch to his raised arm. Clad only in a pink bra and matching panties, she held his eyes and gave him a slow sexy smile.

"You are so beautiful."

Not saying a word, she slowly pulled the strap of her bra down over her right shoulder before twisting around to pull the left one. The straps lay tight and sexy over the tops of her arms when she turned to face him to unhook the lacy piece from behind and slide it off, dropping to the floor next to her dress.

"You like what you see?"

"Katie."

"You have to tell me, yes."

A sound like stone rubbing on stone issued from his throat as he stared at her. He nodded yes while reaching to trace one finger gently over her right breast. Heavy with desire, her nipples stood straight and hard as if at his command, at his touch. She forced in a loud inhaled lungful of air when he finally pulled her hard and rough into him. But instead of slamming her against the wall like she ached for him to do, he lifted her up and carried her into the bedroom. Instead of slamming her down on the bed and tearing her panties off like she wanted, he laid her gently into the mattress and kissed her in a soft, slow way. With such desire, Kate forgot how to breathe. When he released her mouth and finally attacked the surface of her aching breasts with his lips, she arched her back up like a cat and whispered out his name.

His mouth sucked up to the peak of one breast, blowing hot air over the tip of it before he flicked his tongue over the hardened end. Drawing one then the other into his warm mouth, he pushed her traveling hands from him. She moaned out her distress, but he soon silenced that by moving his devouring mouth from her aching breast to her burning wet middle. Her moaning returned as she lifted her bottom up to greet his wet sensual kiss.

Desire, hot and furious moved through her body as his lips worked their magic. She wanted to say stop. She wanted to pull his lips from her middle, and replace it with the hard pulsating penis rubbing fire against her sheets. She needed that hard throbbing erection inside her. Yet the sensation of his mouth and tongue left her aching for more, for so much more, left her wishing the night would never end.

"Oh, Matt."

He raised his head from her.

"No, don't stop." When her moaning softened and the trembling of wanting slowed in her, she pulled at his hair, cradling his cheek with her other hand as she led him to rise above her. She would never regret making love with this man. "Do it now."

"Katie."

"Now." She raised her lower body and shivered as his penis drove hard into her wet core, filling her completely with its enormous length. She begged him with barely spoken words and soft panting sighs to love her before the explosion threatening to erupt within her blacked out all thoughts from her mind. "Oh, yes."

Her wish, her desire. Her dream. He jerked out of her only to thrust hard and fast back inside, causing tremors to build up in her center, to spread outward throughout her entire body as her fierce orgasm roared hot and wet out of her. She lifted up to meet his downward thrust, breasts to chest, hip to hip, mouth to mouth. Mad, hard, grinding, until those tremors subsided and she closed her eyes in satisfied disbelief.

Speaking out her name on a gruff breath, Matt sank one last time into her before stiffening and slowly relaxing. To her, his satisfaction was even more fulfilling.

A few moments later, she found her voice. "Did you like that?" He only breathed against her mussed hair and pulled her to his sweaty body. "Matt?"

"Go to sleep, Kate."

"Did you...?"

"Go to sleep, love."

Kate fell asleep slowly in his arms, afraid to fall asleep at all because he might not be there when she woke in the morning.

And she couldn't handle waking up alone.

Chapter Thirteen

Kate awoke Sunday morning, cold and alone. Her worst nightmare coming to life in the room until a vague memory sneaked into her confused mind: the memory of the man leaning over her speaking something she couldn't quite hear, couldn't quite understand. Dressed only in black tuxedo pants and unbuttoned white shirt, he'd smiled down at her before kissing her with such aching gentleness it left her breathless. Warmth slipped past the coldness as the memory took hold of her senses, and Kate closed her eyes tight to recapture the soft feel of his departing kiss.

Yet he was still gone.

Confusion forced her out of her rumpled bed, lingering apprehension darkening in her mind as she glanced around the room. Everywhere she looked were the signs of their lovemaking. Kate sighed and wrapped her arms around her middle. Why was she so afraid? He didn't leave like all the others, yet still she feared.

Shaking her head against the fear, she stood and turned to stare at the bed. His woodsy scent still lingered in the messed up linen as she threw the sheets and light blanket up to cover the bed. A hint of his aroma clung to the pillow.

Oh, I must be in love.

She smiled at the unbidden thought. "More like in lust."

Hot water flowed down her back a few minutes later; the pulsating heat of it soothing her tensed muscles. She lifted her face to the stream, and laughed.

Oh, but this ache felt so good, so sweet.

Moments later, a different type of chill hardened the ends of her bosom now, tightening the little buds into a sharp point as she walked out of the warm bathroom into the air conditioned cold of the hallway. She wrapped her arms around her chest, covering the exposed areas with her warm skin.

The sudden ringing in the kitchen froze her feet just inside the bedroom door and she stood silent as she debated whether or not to answer the phone.

"Matt?" Racing to the kitchen, unconcerned by her nudity, she grabbed the phone and spoke a breathless hello.

"You've slept with him." Now her lack of clothing did concern her. "You little slut," the whispered voice said.

Trembling started in her hands, spreading in a quick burst down her body and into her weakening legs. She leaned hard into the curved edge of the counter. "I don't—"

"Oh, don't even try to deny it." The tone cut into her psyche. "Oh, but you'll be sorry. I warned you about him."

"He's not that way." Strength flowed back into her legs. "I don't know why you need to lie about him." The woman's laughter drilled into her returning energy, sending it spinning far from her. "You need to stop calling me."

"Or what?" The laughter intensified. "Are you going to call the cops?"

"Yes."

"And what do you think they can do for you?"

What could they do? She only had a few strange phone calls, threatening phone calls, yet she hadn't been hurt in any way.

"He's good, isn't he?" This last question sounded soft on the line, only a moment before a loud click echoed in her ears.

This woman had slept with Matthew Hunter.

When the phone rang again while her mind still wandered over her disturbing conversation, she almost knocked it to the ground. Like a burning iron, she wanted so much to throw the object across the room. The answering machine kicked on before she could pick up the receiver, filling the air around her with a sweet, silly voice. After the beep, she heard that voice again.

"Kate?"

"Oh, Erin, I'm so glad to hear your voice."

Her friend laughed. "You sound out of breath again."

"I've been busy."

"Yeah, and I hope it was with a man." Stopping her comment, Kate was relieved when Erin changed the subject of her conversation. "I called to let you know Jack and I are going to be visiting some of the outlying villages on the island, to study the native culture. My husband is really interested in their habits and lifestyle. He couldn't pass up this chance to view it with his own eyes."

"That sounds like fun—for him."

"Very funny," she said, "I'm interested in finding out about them too." A male whisper sounded in the phone line. "He says he can't wait to meet you."

"And I can't wait to meet him."

"So what's been going on with you?" A gentle hissing sound filled the split second of silence, a loud male laugh. "Getting any...sleep?"

Erin does know something, she sensed. But how can she know anything? "I'm sleeping fine. Why do you ask?"

"I'm just curious about you." Male laughter sounded near the phone again, close enough for the man it belonged to be listening in on their conversation. Jack, Kate supposed. "How are Esther and Grace? Billy and Sally?" Erin paused before adding, "Matt?"

"Everyone is fine." Why wasn't she telling her oldest friend about her feelings for the man; about the greatest sex she'd ever remembered experiencing? Was Erin reading her mind, her mood? Time to change the subject again. "On Wednesday I'm going to go to the playhouse."

The subject change startled the other woman. "So you're still helping out with the group?"

"I've got a lot of time on my hands here." Memories from last night warmed in her, sending her brain racing to remember what she was about to say. The whispery lady tried to intrude, tried to weaken her. "I promised I would take your place as their advisor until you returned."

"You haven't found anything better to do with your time?"

"Do you mean anyone better?"

"Oh, damn." Male laughter once again could be heard clear on the phone line. "Damn fool."

"Erin?"

"I was talking about Jack."

"Really?"

"Of course," she said softly, as her friend dragged in a long loud breath. "Who else would I be talking about?"

"You tell me."

"I wasn't talking about anyone else."

She glanced down at her bare feet. "Did you know you have a naked woman standing in your kitchen?"

"Alone?"

Kate smiled. "So, does this mean I won't be hearing from you for a while?"

"Probably not, but we still plan to be back in California by next Friday, Saturday at the latest." Erin stopped talking for a moment, obviously expecting Kate to comment. When she didn't, Erin added, "That's why I'm calling, to let you know I won't be in touch for a few days. I don't want you worrying about me."

The whispery accusing voice entered Kate's head unexpectedly freezing her feet to the ground. Why the woman's call should raise question in Kate's mind now left her with an unsettling feeling deep inside here. Even with the call from a few minutes ago, Kate knew her friend wouldn't have done what the woman implied happened. Still she needed to hear the truth from Erin. "Is Jack nearby right now?"

"No, he's standing over by the window. Why?"

She lowered her voice. "This is a bit personal, and you don't have to answer it if you don't want but I need to know."

"How personal can it be?" Kate heard the smile in her friend's satisfied tone. "I'm happy, married to a wonderful guy."

And she suddenly felt so cold, so achingly alone.

"Jack and I tell each other everything."

"Even about your past lovers?"

"Well, some things need to be left unsaid. Some things are better left to the imagination."

"Like Matt?"

"Matt?" The question had startled Erin. "What about Matt? He's a good friend." Kate could almost she her friend's emerald green eyes widened in disbelief. "He's great to look at and fun to be around most of the time, but I never slept with him, Kate."

"I just wondered."

"Why would you ask me such a question?"

"I've been getting these strange calls from some woman claiming that you and Matt...got together." Clamping her mouth shut on the rest of her words, she lifted off the chair and walked to the corner of the room. Naked both inside and out now, she felt exposed for believing that damn woman. "Forget about it, Erin."

"You thought I was sleeping with Matt, and you want me to just forget about it?"

165

"It's just that woman who called me sounded so sure about it."

Erin's laughter startled Kate straight up into the corner. "I've my hands full with my new husband, believe me. Matt's all yours if you want him."

Kate sighed.

"You believe me, don't you?"

"Yes," Kate said.

"Well, good," relief sounded clear in her voice, "Are you interested in the man?"

"Yes, I'm interested." More than anything, she thought. Now that she knew that the phone caller had lied, her life shined brighter with brilliant possibilities. It was more than just the memory of the wonderful sex they'd shared last night singing in her soul now. "Oh, I am most definitely interested."

****

Matt stood at the back of the theater building watching the woman interact with his friends and associates. She was everything he'd ever imaged her to be. Sensual, sexy, real—a woman with a voice that could charm the worst tempered man to a woman with the power to make the ugliest person feel good stood like she belonged amongst his friends. She pulled at his senses, making it hard to remember why he'd come to this playhouse, this day.

But the manila envelope she held so close to her breasts sent all those feelings to the background as another more disturbing emotion stormed through him. He'd been a fool to think she was any different than the last actress he'd made the mistake of getting involved. He'd started to believe he'd been wrong about Kate's intentions for coming to California. The way she'd been acting didn't fit his original belief. He'd actually started to allow himself to believe Kate, that she didn't know about all the pressure he was getting from so many people to sign the contract to be a silent part of the show.

But the visit from the producer of her comeback television series changed all that for him. He should be angry with her, but he wasn't.

Shouldn't it hurt more to have given half his heart so easily to another woman who only wanted his money? Shouldn't he be angrier with her for doing it to him? Because when he'd left her bed this morning he'd whispered words he'd promised never to say again, words he hoped she hadn't heard. The 'I love you' slipped out of his mouth as he kissed her good-bye, and before he'd a chance to think over the implication of them. Because he'd loved the woman she used to be for so long, he'd let down his defenses.

Confusion still moved through his mind, unchecked in his heart as he watched her ease among the people as if she belonged there, speaking and laughing with them, helping them tune up their performances with a single word or a soft suggestion. His bewilderment only intensified when he spied the second reason he stood hiding in the shadow of the back seats. Anna looked as lovely as when they'd first met, yet all he saw now was her true ugliness.

Stop it, he thought, resolutely burying the memories deep in his subconscious mind. His eyes fell on Kate once again, on his Katie. Even with evidence mounting against her, he still held a degree of hope she wasn't the same as Anna and that she wasn't using her reputation and body to get what she wanted. Anna had hurt him with her betrayal; Kate had the power to destroy him. More than just his friend, more than just a mere woman he'd spent an incredible night with, she was slowly becoming someone he wanted for eternity.

The intensity of his love had scared him so much he'd needed to get away before she spied it in his eyes. The feelings he'd felt for the woman were the same ones he'd remembered feeling in his dreams, in his youthful fantasy-induced daydreams, feelings that had both confused and thrilled him.

And until he could separate the two sets of emotions, the past with the present, he needed to keep his distance.

The incriminating emails and letters from the director and producers of the television series came at the perfect time. Only a fool in love would deny the proof those letters revealed about her true desires.

He may be half in love with this actress turned lawyer.

But no one ever called Matthew Hunter a fool.

****

The answering machine sounded when Kate stepped into Erin's cool living room an hour after play practice, sending her rushing through the living room to the small kitchen. Hoping to hear her old friend's voice, happiness still warmed her heart in pleasure as Dana, her assistant, chirped a bright hello.

"Hey, Kate, are you there?" A silent pause before Dana said, "I'm just calling to let you know I e-mailed you the information you asked about that gorgeous man's security company. It seems to be a fast growing business. Your guy is buying up smaller security businesses in the Pacific Northwest, with desire to expand into the Midwest or Eastern states. Oh, I left you some web addresses to check out. That man seems..." Another pause filled the air in the kitchen. "That Matt guy seems to go through women like I go through chocolate when I'm PMSing. You know what I mean." Another second of silence before she added, "But it does seem like—"

The answering machine cut off the rest of her message, leaving Kate wondering what she meant to say. This day was only going from bad to worse and she still couldn't find the courage to open that envelope laying on the coffee table in the living room. This one was thinner than the first one Matt had given young Sally, yet it seemed much heavier.

Punching the side of the phone, she walked into the living room and stared at the envelope for a long moment. Matt had seemed confused, unsure when he'd handed it to Sally. A visible hint of temper lined the edges of his mouth.

"No, I'll look at you later." Going into Erin's office just off the living room, Kate reached over and turned on the computer before stepping out to change into something cooler. With the coffee brewing in the kitchen a few minutes later, she wandered back into the cramped office area and settled at the desk. Kate ignored the spam collection of e-mail and opened one from Dana. The attachment revealed the extent of Matt's holdings. He was very well off. It didn't really interest her, so she quickly logged into one of the gossip websites Dana had left. A disreputable tabloid-like site affiliated with an even more disreputable newspaper. Why she checked it out she would never understand. And after reading all the archived articles about one certain playboy named Matthew Hunter, she wished she had left well enough alone.

But one article leaped up to greet her with an unexpected thrill. This one spoke of a rumored past fantasy relationship between Matt and a well-known actress of the nineties. No name was given for the actress but for obvious reasons Katherine Adams came to mind. According to the article, the young Matt had a horrible crush on this one particular actress and the writer of the story said he had proof of his strange attachment to the woman.

"What?" She spoke out loud. "I didn't notice any proof." Leaping up to the beginning of the article, she wrote down the name of the reporter and the date. The man wrote the article in May of 1999, two years after she'd gotten out of the business, one year after her life-changing marriage started to fall apart.

No, she wasn't going to think of Bruce now. As

she scrolled down the list of articles written by that reporter about Matt, only one more mentioned his fantasy love involvement with the unnamed woman. No letters, no proof of any kind.

Kate relaxed into the chair. Why was she getting so upset over an article written by an unknown writer for a disreputable newspaper? This particular tabloid had been sued by more than one well-known person for publishing outrageous lies.

But it was fun to read.

Could he feel her heartbeat roaring in her chest beneath that aroused area? Could he sense the breath locked deep in her lungs, fighting to get free?

Mail truck, thankfully the digitally enhanced voice from the computer broke through her unwanted memories.

This e-mail was from Dana.

Kate,

Did you get the info I sent about Hunter's company? Your guy is buying off many small to medium sized security firms in your area and, from what I've read all the transactions have gone smoothly. Everyone seems satisfied with the deals. He's in the process of moving TopNotch's headquarters to your area.

Oh, and for your eyes only, TopNotch has requested to search our financial records. I expected this, but they seem to be focusing on Bruce's—rather on your—personal financial history. What do you want me to do?"

Dana

Temper erupted in Kate like a fierce volcano inside a high mountain. *How dare that man check up on Bruce?*

She quickly typed her reply.

Dana,

Do not let that man get anything personal about Bruce. It was Williams, Williams, Gay & Brown that sent out the request for information on his firm not my husband. I'll find out what Matt's up to on this end.

Kate

Slamming the send button with a little more force than necessary, she dragged in one angry breath after another as she waited for her assistant's reply. When she read it a mere two minutes later, slight fear mixed with her broiling anger. Bruce's information had been released to TopNotch Security, Inc.

"Bastard."

The digital voice spoke out again, and she opened her new e-mail without thinking—and froze in her seat.

I want you on your knees in front of me, devouring my dick with your talented mouth. You'll suck it rough and hard until I cum all over your mouth.

She quickly closed that message and opened the next one on the list. And she wished she just deleted it too. *After I pull my cock out of your pussy I'd slam you over and stick it right up your ass. You'll scream for me, bitch.*

"Oh, my Lord," she whispered in disgusted disbelief. "These are just like Erin's stalker letters."

Reading the rest of the message, not wanting to read but doing it anyway, she saved them all to the CD drive and disconnected the computer, the last message still lingering in her mind.

These are only a sample of my dreams with you. I'm hoping to make them a reality someday, Katherine Adams, even if it takes forever.

Your biggest fan,

Matt

"Oh, Matt," she sighed in the suddenly quiet air of the cramped office, "I guess you got your wish."

****

Two hours later, Kate was still in a foul mood. Such a mood she didn't look anywhere except straight ahead as she walked toward the house next door.

"Hello, Kate," Esther said, opening the front door of her home. "Come on in."

"It's good to see you, Esther."

"Don't just stand there, dear," she added, pulling her into the warm entry of her home. "Dinner is almost ready."

An innocent smile and bright shining glance stared into her as she walked past the smaller woman. A tingling sensation formed deep in Kate's throat. She twisted around and started back toward the door, but the second elderly woman's tight grip on her upper arm stopped her forward momentum.

Matt stood in the kitchen doorway.

She should have realized the man would be here.

Oh, why didn't she see his car?

"Why don't the two of you go into the living room and sit down," Esther said easily, "while Grace and I get dinner on the table."

Matt glared at her from across the bright room, a closed look that hurt her more than any words, as if they'd never been together; as if they'd never made love. Kate read all of those emotions in his cold expression. An ache so cutting, so deep, pierced into her chest.

And why shouldn't she hurt? Didn't she just read five or six of the most disgusting emails she'd ever received? He'd sent those emails to her, a copy of the letters he'd written when he was a young man.

Yet Kate wouldn't give him the satisfaction of seeing how hurt she truly was. Kate Williams disappeared; replaced by Katherine Adams. If he wanted her older self, she would give him her older self. Deepening her voice into her trademark breathy alto, she said, "I didn't expect you to be here. It seems your dear sweet mother is playing games with us again."

His blank eyes widened, a hint of heat burned out of them. "Katherine?"

"Katherine?" The small woman glared from one to the other before settling puzzled dark eyes on her silent friend. "Matt, this is Kate not Katherine."

"No, she is Katherine." Bitterness sounded in his voice now. "You can change your name but not who you are."

"Boy, what are you babbling about now?"

"Ask her, Aunt Grace." Pointing his flashing eyes toward her, Kate stepped backward at the force of his stare. "Ask her why she's seeking information about me and TopNotch Security even after I told her I wasn't interested in funding her damn comeback into acting? Ask her why she told everyone involved with 'Three Sisters' that I'd agreed to be a sponsor, why I'm receiving information about the show from its producers and director."

His accusation hurt more than she thought possible, but the core of her that'd borne more than her share of pain stepped in to help. "You're so convinced I'm after your money, aren't you? Did you ever stop to think I might be after you? Body and soul? Maybe I want the guy who—" Slamming her mouth against her harsh statement, she ripped the words from her heart too. Why accuse him of being a possible stalker when she wasn't even sure she was the actress the writer was referring too? It could've just as easily have been Erin.

No, it was her. Hadn't he admitted it to her earlier?

"Who what, Katherine?" he asked darkly. "Finish your sentence." He reached out to her and clamped hard fingers around her upper arms, jerking her tight to his heaving chest. She stood straight and tall, frozen like a statue. "Maybe you want the guy who what?"

"Get your damn hands off of me."

His fingers bit into hers, pulling her even tighter

173

to him. Even now, in anger, he wanted her. Scaring her, confusing her, the words he whispered out softly to her that same morning rang clear in her ears.

No, this man would have never said those words.

"Boy, you're hurting the girl." Grace's loud voice mixing with Esther's quieter one finally penetrated the man's fierce demeanor. His hand dropped hard to his side.

Between the two women Kate found her body moving away from his rigid form. She only stared at him; afraid to look too deeply into his downward angled face, so she only stared at her clasped hands. What would she see there? What would she read in his eyes now?

And what had happened to make him change from thinking he loved her to acting like he hated her? Or had she only imagined she'd heard those words?

She needed to get away, away from the confusion and pain this man brought to her body, her mind, to her soul.

But it was Matt who spoke up. "Mom, I need to go."

"I think you'd better." His aunt glared at him while encircling a heavy arm around her sagging shoulders. "You've done enough damage for one day, don't you think?"

"It's my fault," whispered Kate. "I'm to blame."

"No, girl, don't go there." Her arm tightened around her shoulders harder, pulling her face gently against her soft chest. "This boy doesn't know a good thing when he sees it."

"I'm going now," he said.

Kate looked straight into his blank eyes and spied something warm and inviting hidden deep within them before his angry emptiness returned.

"But you haven't eaten yet," his mother said.

"I'm really not all that hungry right now."

"Boy, you're killing your mother acting this way."

"I know I am, Aunt Grace." His blank glance never left her. A part of her ached with a burning pain as he left the room and walked out the front door, yet she didn't feel total despair. Like a woman hanging onto a rubber boat in the middle of a storm-tossed sea, she held onto the brief glimpse of warmth flashing from his glance.

"Dear?"

Looking toward the smaller woman Kate pulled her glance away from the closed door. "I'm all right, Esther. Your son and I had a little...disagreement."

"The boy's nuts," Grace said.

"Be quiet," Esther said.

"You know I'm right." Grace dropped her hand from Kate's arm and moved from her frigid body. Sinking into the comfortable seat of the couch, she added, "He's acting like a crazy man, refusing to see what is so clear to see."

"The past and the present are sometimes hard to reconcile."

"Bullshit, Esther."

"Did your son see all of my movies?" The question came out before she had a chance to think of the implication of its answer. "Did he ever mention me when he was growing up?"

At the startled looks leaping between the two elderly women the answer to her question was clear.

"He did see my movies?" So the story she'd read in that tabloid was the truth—those disgusting emails—and she was the woman that writer mentioned in it. It made her feel strange and exhilarated at the same time, sad and used. A fantasy fulfilled by the man the boy had grown-up to become. Those emails proved that. "I read this article about Matt on a website today, stating he'd fantasized about a certain actress when he was younger. That actress was me, wasn't it?"

"Dear?"

"You shouldn't believe everything you read, girl."

"I don't normally pay attention to those types of things, Grace." Sitting down beside the larger woman, she watched as Matt's mom sat in the recliner in front of them. "But Matt's acting strange. We're—"

"Kate, answer me one question."

"If I can, Esther," she said.

"Have you and my son ever been intimate?"

"What?"

"I'm not judging you, dear." Her eyes shined kindness and concern. "I know it's none of my business but...I need to know if the two of you've made love."

A flush moved over the flesh of her face, giving the older woman the answer she wanted without Kate saying a word. She said, "It was a mistake."

"Girl, you should have thought of that before you leaped into bed with him."

"Dear?" Kate allowed the smaller woman to pull her clamped hands from her lap and cradled them in her own. She was beginning to fall in love with this sweet, kind-hearted woman, almost as much as the son she'd held in that tiny womb. "Why do you think it was a mistake?"

"This conversation seems so unreal." Kate muttered under her breath. "Unreal."

"Why does it feel so unreal to you?" The woman smiled at her, diamond-like sparkles shining deep in her eyes. "Is it because I'm talking to you about sex?"

"No, it's not that." Kate sucked her lower lip into her mouth and rubbed her teeth over it, allowing the biting pressure to ease her mind. She grabbed onto a less threatening topic of conversation. "My mother would never want to know about my love life. It just wouldn't be part of our normal conversations."

"I'm not that way."

Did it matter anyway? Kate had slept with this woman's son not even a month after meeting him. Who was she to judge someone else's behavior? "You must think I'm the worst kind of person for sleeping with your son weeks after meeting him."

"I don't think that at all."

"I would if I were you, Esther."

"Girl, some of the women he dated didn't even last after the second date."

Kate smiled at the big woman. "According to the tabloids, he's been a pretty busy guy."

"My son has a way with women."

"I've noticed that," replied Kate. "He's hard...to ignore."

"He has a way about him that attracts all sorts of women."

"Thanks, Esther."

"For what, dear?"

"For not treating me like some kind of tramp." She leaned toward the older woman, wrapping her fingers around her warm hand. "I don't feel like such a fool now. At least now I know my heart wasn't the first one he'd broken; and it probably won't be the last."

Another look past between the two older women and Kate frowned at the mixture of puzzlement, of a question asked and answered, clear on their faces.

"But you know what really seems strange?" She ignored their looks, ignored their unusual quietness. "While looking through those tabloid articles, I didn't see any mention of Matt and Anna."

"Her?" Kate sliced her eyes toward the larger woman, moving a bit away from her tightening embrace. "That witch."

"Witch?" Startled, Kate glanced from Grace to Esther. "I got the impression from Emily that he was broken when Anna left him."

"Is that what that witch is telling everyone?"

"It was only my impression, but—yes."

"Girl, don't you believe it."

Relief breathed sudden warmth in her. "Are you saying she lied?"

"Dear, she's the reason why my son is so angry at you and Erin for asking him to finance that damn television pilot."

"I don't understand." Kate sat quiet, hands raised in the air in confusion. "I can see why he'd be angry at Erin; I'm mad at her in a way too. We were supposed to discuss this opportunity while I was here this month, but I found out she'd already sighed on to it. I haven't even read the script yet. He shouldn't be upset with me."

"It's not you," Esther said, adding, "Or Erin."

"It's that damn witch," Grace added with vigor. "It's that Anna."

Chapter Fourteen

"What did Anna do that was so bad?" Kate leaned toward the woman in the chair. "Why would that make your son want to hurt me?"

"My son doesn't want to hurt you."

Ignoring her comment for fear of saying something she might regret, she only repeated her questions. Remembering the way he'd acted the second time they'd actually talked, she added, "Is that why he accused me of sending that script to him? Is that why he's accused me of trying to use my...body to get him to fund the project? He gave me the script plus I have another envelope full of emails and messages. I haven't even looked at those yet."

"He's crazy."

"Grace?"

"You know I'm right." Grace leaned toward Esther. "That boy of yours is blind."

"We all warned him about her." Grace looked into her eyes now. "Anna—that witch—made him believe many lies."

"Lies?" Kate wanted to know about his relationship with the woman yet she didn't. She heard so much conflicting information about it. Was he still in love with her? Is she the reason he'd made love to her than acted as if it never happened? She needed the truth, yet she didn't want to know.

She already hurt too much.

"My son believed she was falling in love with him."

"The witch," said Grace.

Ignoring her, Kate leaned closer to Esther. "But

she wasn't?"

"No, she wasn't." Sadness sounded in her voice, a fierce pain that only a loving mother could feel. "She used his loneliness against him."

"From the stories I've read, how can you believe he was ever lonely?" Kate sighed and sat back in her chair. "According to the gossip website I visited, Matt's had a different woman every few months or so. I doubt she used his loneliness to get her way with him."

"The boy has been lonely all his life," Grace said.

"How can you say that?"

"When you don't have love, dear," Esther reached a gentle hand to her, placing it soft on her bare leg. "You can feel very alone."

"Yes." Kate knew that by experience. For eight years she'd lived a fairy tale life to the outside world that turned into a cold loveless reality when the front door closed. "I know what it's like to feel alone."

The women just looked at each other. She glanced from one woman to the other, feeling their concern for her, for Matt. Wrapping herself up in the warmth of their wide open emotions would give her so much joy, but she wouldn't do it. She wouldn't do it because she would only hurt more when she left California.

And leave she meant to do.

"Anna sensed his weakness." Esther's words flowed in the chilled air, and Kate concentrated hard on them. "I think we all thought Matt had fallen in love with your friend, but—"

"With Erin?" Her feelings sprang out of control at the words, sadness moved through her. "That's why the stories about his exploits with women ended three years ago. That is so sad for him."

"No, you've got it all wrong," Grace said.

"Yes, Grace, that's it exactly. Poor Matt." Her heart hurt for the man's unrequited love but along with the grief poured a large dose of jealousy.

Jealousy? Was he thinking of Erin when he made love to her? Was he thinking of Anna?

Or was she way off base with this?

"Erin's married, you know," she said quickly.

This comment jerked both of their glances toward her. Grace found her voice first, "Erin and Jack are married?"

Kate nodded at the heavy woman beside her.

"That's great!"

"Great?" She stared aghast at the smirking woman, confused by her beaming smile. "How can you say that when your best friend's son's heart is bleeding?"

"It wasn't his heart that was bleeding."

"Grace, be still," Esther said.

Another secret passed between them, one Kate wished she could read because this whole situation with Erin and Matt confused her beyond reason. She trusted Erin, and believed her when she'd said nothing had happened between them, yet—

"Grace and I were telling you about Matt and Anna's short relationship." Placing her open palm on her legs, Esther stretched her fingers wide against her jean-clad leg. "I'll admit that my son started seeing Anna after he found out about Erin's relationship with the professor, but he was happy for her."

"If he was so happy why did he start dating such a bi...witch?"

Grace grinned. "The other word fit her better."

"He didn't love Anna," his mother continued, "He fooled himself into thinking he did. He wanted something that he never had. A family, maybe."

"How can a man like Matt want a family?" Kate glanced at her. "He doesn't seem the type."

"You've got him all wrong," Esther said.

"I don't think so."

Silence moved through the room, a heavy sad quietness that pulled at Kate.

181

"Anna?" Desperate to break up the unnerving silence, Kate asked, "You were going to tell me what Anna did to him. I take it she didn't want children."

Esther looked deep into her eyes before looking down to the floor. "I guess it won't hurt you to find out the truth."

Kate waited until Esther lifted up her head. "Anna started dating him, hoping he would fall in love with her. He wanted to love someone, to be a part of something stronger than a brief fling, so he allowed her inside his defenses. He even asked her to marry him."

"So what I heard was true?"

"No, it wasn't true."

"Esther, I'll take over now." Grace moved half off the sofa to stare at Kate. "After Matt asked her to marry him, the witch started pressuring him about financing this movie she was involved with. It would have been her big break, like 'Midnight Revenge' was yours. He was actually thinking about going against his principles. Until he found her in a, let's just say, very compromising position with the director."

"He caught her with another man?" Kate couldn't believe it. She may have been ashamed of making love to the man only a few weeks after meeting him, but she would never forget the experience. No man ever came close to satisfying her like Matt satisfied her, and she was sure no one ever would again. "What a fool!"

Grace smiled; more at the expression on her face than her actual words. Like her thoughts had been written on her forehead for all to see.

"As you could guess, the boy decided against financing that movie." Grace leaned closer to her. "And the marriage."

"Poor Matt."

"My son didn't love Anna." The smaller woman rose from her chair and stretched out her hand.

"Come on, I need to show you something."

"Esther, do you think that's a good ideal?"

"Grace, it's time all of this is out in the open."

"And what will Matt say when he finds out?"

For a moment, Esther froze as her thoughts seemed to leap from one thing to another but in the end she still helped Kate up with her tight grip and pulled her toward the hallway.

Kate let the older woman lead her out of the living room. They stopped at the same doorway Kate had escaped into the night of the strange phone call; the night Matt first showed her his feelings. The door opened and she walked in ahead of the women. This time she saw the room for what it was, a well-maintained storage area.

"Wait here, dear."

"What do you want me to see?"

Esther didn't answer. Kate watched as the small woman walked toward two neatly stacked sets of boxes in the far corner of the tiny room, picking up the top one from the nearest pile. She opened it and pulled out a bunch of books and bundled papers from it. "Oh, no."

"Esther, what's wrong?"

"The letters are gone." Frantic now, the woman pushed the box away and tore opened the one on top of the second neat stack. "Where can they be?"

"Esther," Kate froze just inside the doorway, "Grace? What's going on here? What letters are missing?"

Both of the women ignored her as they looked at each other, fear shining bright and clear in their wide-open eyes.

****

Kate watched Matt drive away from his mother's house around ten that next night. He didn't bother looking toward the front window where she was standing, were she'd been standing for the last hour or so. She'd waited behind the questionable protection of the thick white curtains, in the same spot, staring out this same window, for most of the day.

Pathetic, she thought.

"Oh, stop it," she said, pulling the drapes shut and sitting lightly on the couch.

Thankfully another image took the place of Matt's, the image of an elderly woman with a fearful expression shining clear from her eyes.

What letters did Esther want her to see anyway? What journal did she want her to read? Were they the original of those disgusting emails she'd received? Or were they even worse?

A mystery, she thought.

Pulling in a few quick deep breaths to calm her intense emotions, she walked to the kitchen sink and splashed chilled water on her face before grabbing a dishtowel and drying her skin as she made her way to the office. She'd intended to read over a copy of the script for "The Sound of Music" but her hands fastened onto the television script instead.

Matt thought the only reason she'd come to visit Erin was because of this movie, so she figured she might as well read it. She doubted she'd be able to get any sleep tonight.

Settling deep into the plush white recliner, she tucked her legs under her and opened the pages. Her mind quickly closed off the image of Matt's naked body as the story of the three different sisters came to life. Perfect, she thought. The story line of the oldest sister could be the story of her life—a farce of a marriage with a man who had a hard time touching you.

Perfect.

After reading to the last page, she sighed and glanced toward the window. Darkness greeted her sleepy look as a thought formed clear in her mind. She would do this movie. As sleep overtook her, this knowledge was the last thing she remembered. And it was still in her mind when she awakened hours later.

Jerking her body up and out of the chair, she retrieved the fallen script from the floor before glancing at the digital clock on the stand beside the couch.

"That can't be the right time." The clock read ten in the morning.

But when she stood and put all her weight on her numbed legs, she moaned and clamped her fist around the back of the chair. Placing both feet flat on the floor, she glanced down again to make sure they were truly on the floor before she gingerly moved a half step, dragging her feet toward the kitchen. Her stiff legs trembled as she moved them in front of her. From no feeling in her lower extremities to a biting, tingling sharp one as blood rushed back through her legs and into her numbed feet. She straightened up to her full height.

"Damn." Why had she fallen asleep in that cramp position anyway? "Damn."

She grabbed the back of the white couch and waited as the stinging sensation faded from her legs a bit before stepping another ginger half-step toward the kitchen and Erin's phone. Her cell, sitting on the stand beside the guest bed, seemed way too far away right now. The kitchen was so much closer.

The tingling faded a step at a time, and all feeling returned to her legs and feet by the time she reached the kitchen counter and picked up the phone. Hopefully Erin still had that old agent's number nearby. Placing the phone back into its cradle, she searched through a small drawer under the phone and found a pink-colored phone book. The number she wanted was on one of the last pages. She waited for a few minutes, listening to the ringing tone of it, before a deep-voiced female answered with a cheery hello.

"Is Bill in?" Kate asked, "This is Kate Williams.

I need to talk to him about a television program he's casting for."

"Oh," the woman said, "You mean, *Three Sisters*."

"Yes."

Silence filled the phone line. "He's not in right now. I could give him a message."

"That'll be fine." Kate gave the woman both her cell number and Erin's home phone before saying, "Let him know that I finally read the script. I'm interested in being a part of the show."

"Mrs. Williams?" A clicking sound moved through the phone line. "Oh, you're Katherine Adams, or you used to be."

Kate laughed. "Well, I guess I still am, in a way." And with sudden inspiration, she declared, "I guess I can't get past that simple fact."

"A little older, a little wiser," she said. "I'll let Bill know you've called. He was only waiting on your yes to get everything started."

"So, Erin did already sign her contract to do the show?"

"Last month."

Kate heard the smile in the receptionist's bright tone.

"I think this show is going to be a big hit. It can't miss with one of the hottest names in the business now and two comebacks."

"The story is a good one," Kate agreed. "There does seem to be a lot of angst for the director to work with, with those three troubling sisters and their horrible relationships."

"The stories of a woman's life," she said lightly.

"Yes."

"Bill will be happy when I give him your message."

Hanging up the phone, relief turned to happiness as the opportunity to be a part of such a high-class show finally formed completely in her mind. And excitement. For a long time, she hadn't been excited about anything. But now—

Now if only she could get her love life back on track too, her world would be one of complete bliss.

Chapter Fifteen

Matt's BMW was parked in his mother's driveway when Kate returned from a very unproductive play practice the same day. Between Anna's attitude, Sally's pouting, and Emily's unusual pissy mood, she was glad to be back in Erin's cool house. If Joe and his son hadn't finished painting the background mountains scene for the play, the whole day would have been a complete bust.

This small town rendition of the well-known musical might be the worst performance anywhere, but at least the background would look good. And seeing Billy so happy after hearing all the compliments was priceless to her.

Kate was going to miss these wonderful people when she returned to Seattle in a few weeks. Shaking the tearful feelings away, she kicked off her shoes and slammed her old canvas bag onto the couch. The answering machine beeped a harsh tone from the kitchen, sending her racing toward the bright room. As she swept past the stand beside the couch, the accusing manila envelope fell to the floor and she stared at it for a few seconds before ignoring it and speeding to the kitchen.

She didn't know exactly what was in that thing, but she had a feeling it involved "Three Sisters."

And she wasn't in the mood right now for that.

The answering machine beeped a second time.

"Bill?"

She pressed the play button on the machine and skipped past three messages left from Erin's students until she heard the gruff voice of her old agent, as rough sounding as ever. She smiled in remembrance.

"Katherine. I mean, Kate. Thanks for getting back to me. I'm glad you've decided to do the show. I'll get the contract ready. Talk to you later."

A knock on the front door interrupted the short message, sending her speeding toward the door and opening it before she thought to ask who was there.

She should've asked.

"Hello, Kate."

"Matt?"

But before he could say anything else, another familiar voice from the phone sent her racing back to the kitchen. She knew this voice. She's heard it at least one time before. But who was she?

"I see you haven't taken my advice. He was there with you, wasn't he? He's using you the same way he used your friend and me..." Biting anger deepened the whispered voice. "But I guess you'll have to live with your mistakes."

Matt entered the kitchen and leaned against the doorframe. "What's going on?"

She pressed her finger to her lips for him to continue listening.

"Those two old ladies have been filling you..."

Her head shot up as Anna's face formed in her mind, but Matt said her name first. "Anna!"

"Why is she telling me lies about you?" Startled eyes lifted to his dark face. Anger burned the silver color of his eyes black. "I've done nothing to her."

"The bitch!" A slight smile tried to lift up the frown off his mouth. "Is she the one who's been calling you all along?"

Only nodding, she turned back to look at the phone.

Anna whispered. "He's good at filling a woman's head with lies."

Kate didn't look at him.

189

"He's done the right thing by my dad, so I'll not be calling you anymore." Silence, a pause where Matt softly said TopNotch Security before she warned, "One last bit of advice—remember those emails."

Silence spoke loud after the message ended, a silence that she didn't want to fill up with unnecessary words.

Remember those emails.

"Do you believe her, Katie?"

Kate stared at him now. "Do I believe her about what?"

"About me."

Confusion stole into her mind, so profound and yet so simple, clamored inside her head. "I don't know what I believe anymore. I've read those emails, copies of some of your more descriptive letters to me."

"How did you get my letters?"

"I don't have the originals. Someone emailed me parts of them." She allowed her voice to lower seductively and her eyes to linger hot on his. "I don't think you've been completely truthful with me about everything, Matt. You've told me about the letters, but you made me believe they were innocent and sweet."

He swallowed hard, stiffening up a bit at her changing approach. "They were sweet."

"Oh, were they?" She stepped closer, tracing a finger along the edge of his shirt buttons. "Would you like to read some things I received recently? I printed them out."

"Katie?"

"Or maybe you'd like me to act out a few of your favorite fantasies for you." She wrapped her arms around his waist, stepping tight to him. "Would you like to do that?"

"Katie!"

Her hand slid up his back and over his shoulder,

settling on the middle button of his gray dress shirt, and she leaned closer. "Do you still want me?"

His breath exhaled loud and mint-smelling against her face, a tingling experience that left her holding onto her own breath. "What?"

"Do you still want me to make your fantasy come true?"

"No." His eyes darkened, his voice deepened in a rough, strangely exhilarating way. "You've already fulfilled my boyhood fantasy."

"Oh, but those emails claimed you wanted so much more."

"Katie?" He stepped back from her, glared at her stilled body for a long moment. "I don't want you this way."

"Answer my question." Heart beating fast in her own chest, she grabbed the ends of her bright green tee with crossed arms and lifted it over her head. "Do you still want me?"

"Kate, don't." His eyes darkened almost black again as he watched her. "Please...."

"Please what, Matt?" Opening the button and pulling down the zipper of her jeans, she let them drop to her feet and stepped out. "Please let me make love to you? Please make love to me? Please make my fantasy come true? Or please stop?"

He moaned out her name.

"I hope it's not the last choice." Her seduction of him was seducing her. The weakness in her legs, the harshness of her sharp breaths, the rapid beat of her overworked heart told her he wasn't the only one hurting. "I want you, Matt."

"Katie, I'm leaving tomorrow."

She stopped her caressing hands as she slid the middle button of his shirt open and touched the warmth of his tanned skin. His confession hurt yet she still wanted him. It didn't matter if she never saw him again. Tonight she would build a lifetime of memories to get her through the lonely years. "But you can still have me tonight." Stepping back away from him, she pulled his shirt apart with one hard movement, hearing the buttons pop and land with tiny clinks around the kitchen floor. "And I still want you."

"I'm only here because my mom said I should come to tell you that I was leaving."

"And you've told me."

Reaching behind her, she unhooked her bra and let it drop to the floor at her feet. "Tell me you don't want me, Matt, and I'll put all my clothes back on."

"Katie, I want you."

Yet he stood straight and still in front of her, almost afraid to move to her, to touch her, she sensed. Oh, but she so needed him to touch her. Like she needed him in her dreams, those dreams where she was a sexually exciting woman again.

"Oh, I see how it's to be." Grinning she moved toward him and placed her palms over the hardened nipples of his tight chest. "You feel so nice."

He grunted, still standing like a statue, so tall and strong in front of her.

Enjoying the game now, she ran the tips of her nails down his chest then back up again until her fingers were once again encircling those tight buds. Her own breasts hardened in aching need as her heart raced under them. Her right hand lifted from his chest to caress slow and easy over her left breast, flicking over the tight edge of it with a moan.

"Oh, Katie." His body trembled under her smoothing touch, grieving eyes shining as he watched her other hand play around her body. She cupped her right breast and caressed a wet finger over her nipple. Oh, it felt so good.

"Matt." Dropping her hand, she settled both of them around his waist and moved her fingers under his waistband. He groaned when her thumb and index finger undid the button and slid inside, and then down. At the touch of her hand against his hardened cock, she raised her head and kissed his mouth, slow and soft. She encircled her fingers around him, squeezing him gently. "Aren't you going to kiss me back?"

And his control broke at her question.

Wrapping her up in his arms, he deepened the kiss and thrust his tongue into her mouth. A groan escaped his throat when he pulled his mouth away from her lips and stared into her eyes. She must have shown him what he searched so hard to see because suddenly his mouth dropped with a hunger like none she'd ever known before, hard and demanding back to hers.

Oh, how the man could kiss, she thought for a brief moment before he pushed her head back and buried his face into her throat, sending her heart leaping out of her chest and trapping her breath tight in her lungs. His lips traveled beyond her face to capture the same heavy nipple she'd been touching earlier, licking it with rough wetness.

Could he feel her heartbeat roaring in her chest beneath that aroused area? Could he sense the breath locked deep in her lungs, fighting to get free?

When he moved his devouring mouth from one nipple to the other, he lifted her up easy into his arms, causing her to release his pulsating erection. Deep rushing need raced into her, wetting the area between her legs with delicate warmth. A need so fierce, so electric, so overwhelming entered that area as his hand roamed down the length of her upper body to settle gently against the soft cotton-lined material covering her moist center.

But no, she wanted to seduce him now. She wanted him to ache and need her beyond measure. She needed to give him his fantasy. Maybe because it would leave him room to realize it wasn't really that actress he truly desired, but the total woman she was now.

Sighing as his finger slipped into the top of her

tiny panties, as he carried her into the living room, she almost allowed him the opportunity to overtake her senses. She moved his hands gently away when he settled her into the sofa beside him. Then she rose up from the seat to kneel on the floor between his spreading legs. His dark eyes closed as he laid his head full of short blondish-brown hair against the white sofa. And waited, she sensed, waited with inhaled breath caught in his tight lungs, with a heart hammering out of control inside his own chest, for her to fulfill a more basic boyhood fantasy. She sensed his physical reactions as she stared hot at him.

"Matt." She wanted him to look at her. "Matt."

"Kate."Not Katie now, but Kate. How soon before he would call her Katherine? Oh, she didn't want him to call her Katherine. Now, as she placed her hands onto the opening of his pants, as she pulled the zipper the rest of the way down with ease, she *was* Katherine Adams. The actress the tabloids said could still the hearts of men from fifteen to fifty.

Matt was making love to who she used to be.

And she didn't care.

"Lift up your hips." His pants slid down easily over his lean hips and long legs. His legs felt so hard and firm against the tips of her fingers, the tiny blonde hairs standing on end. Her palms moved slowly over that rough skin as she pushed his pants and boxers down to his ankles before tugging them off his bared feet. When had he stepped out of his shoes, she wondered with a smile. She traveled her fingers back up his legs, encircling them over his thighs before she breezed a heated breath at his throbbing cock. He sighed and whispered out words she couldn't quite hear.

"Do you want me to touch you?"

"Damn."

"Is that a yes?" He leaned forward and grabbed the back of her head with such force it made a smile

194

peek from around her mouth. "I guess it's a yes."

He jerked his bottom upward when her mouth encircled him, falling backward against the sofa a few strokes later. She felt the wet warmth from her middle soaking her panties as if his mouth was devouring her instead of her pleasuring him. She had never wanted to please a man more, never wanted to satisfy a man more.

He was leaving, and she would never see him again. This time with him would have to last her a lifetime because she sensed deep down beyond the sexual desire that this was more than just two people taking pleasure only.

This was much more than just simple sex.

"Kate." He pulled her head up with a groan and lifted her from her knees, settling her on his feet in front of him. His mouth didn't touch her like she wanted and his fingers only briefly pressed into her middle as he tore off the last barrier preventing him from seeing her, but a second later the disappointment roared from her mind as he lifted her to his lap and buried his hardness deep into her.

"Oh, Matt." Taking her with such pressure, with such force, she could only wrap her arms around his back and jerk her body up and down in time with him. Like two animals coupling in a field, two people making love.

With almost unbearable need, she sank her nails into the back of his head and pulled at his hair, drawing his mouth up to hers. With one more almost hurtful thrust, she felt his release shooting deep into her, caught his rushing exhaled breath within her mouth before her own answering response built and released within her like small waves miles in the Pacific, building until they crashed onto the shore.

"Kate."

"Matt." He sank weak into the sofa and pulled her down on top of him. Sweat poured from his heavy body, bathing her with his unique scent, but she didn't push him away. She never wanted to push him away, never wanted him to leave her. "Oh, Matt."

"Kate?" A single tear slid down from her eyes, moving along the curve of her cheek before dropping onto the sofa under him. A single tear.

"Kate?"

"Let me go."

"What's wrong?"

Suddenly the mistake she'd just made tore into her heart, breaking it into a million pieces. "You're leaving."

"Yes, but—"

"I'll be going back to Seattle soon." When he didn't release her, she pushed at his chest. "I thought I'd be alright with making love to you. Even knowing you're leaving and not coming back, I thought I could handle it. I was wrong."

"Katie?"

"Now it's back to Katie?" Another tear formed in her eyes, but she forced it back. His gray eyes stared into her face, studying her with such confusion. "When you closed your eyes who were you thinking of?"

Anger burned out in those eyes now, blocking out all the confused tenderness she'd been reading in them. Now only blankness showed, a blank emptiness that hurt her more than anything.

"Who do you think I was thinking of?" Jerking up from beneath her, he moved away from the couch. "I don't understand you."

"Were you making love to the woman you fantasized about when you were a teenager—or me?"

"Oh, dear Lord." Swerving toward her he stood tall and straight, naked and magical. "Katherine Adams and Kate Williams are one and the same person—you. I made love to *you*."

"You don't understand."

"No, Katie," his tone was gentle now. "*You* don't

196

understand. Yes, I had a major crush on you when I was younger. I did write you fan letters that, except for the last one, I never sent."

"Erin's stalker sent her his letters? If you'd read those disgusting letters, you would've gotten sick. Your letters weren't that different." Staring at the fierce burning disbelief heating in his eyes, she almost stopped speaking. She should've stopped speaking. "Erin was so frightened by that bastard that she had to get out of the business. I should be grateful you never sent me your letters."

"Is that how you think of me? You believe those emails you received were...what I'd written years ago."

"I shouldn't have allowed this to happen." With sadness so penetrating it hurt her soul, she stood from the sofa and gathered up her discarded clothes. Pulling on her jeans and shirt, she said, "I thought I could handle being 'Monica' for you, but I was wrong. She's only a character I brought to life in a movie, not me. She was never me."

"No, Katie." Sadness lowered his rough voice an octave. "Every character you've ever developed had a part of you in them."

"No."

Matt only stared at her with those same grief-filled eyes while he dressed and strode to the front door. She wanted to run and plaster her body against it, but it was too late. She'd accused him of being a stalker. She shouldn't be surprised by his leaving her.

She should be surprised if he stayed.

"Katie, I needed an outlet to help me get over the loss of my father. For some reason that outlet was actress named Katherine Adams." His hand settled on the knob but before he turned it he looked back at her. "I should thank you for that. Yes, I did feel something warm for you, but that feeling wasn't even close to the one I'm feeling for you now."

"Matt?"

"I'll be leaving tomorrow, Kate." His deep voice softened. "I'm moving my operation to the old Hotchkiss location here. When you realize you love me, I'll be there."

Opening the door, he didn't look back as he left the house. She could've called him back; she didn't.

****

Kate's tears wouldn't stop flowing. Every time she walked into the living room and glanced at the sofa, her eyes welled up with wetness once again. And when she spied him through a crack in her closed-up curtains going into or out of his mother home the next morning, she couldn't help but feel her heart break into a million tiny pieces. How many times could a heart break before it was impossible to glue all the pieces back together? Kate had a sense she was going to find out.

Somehow she'd managed to get through the first hours after he'd driven away. Somehow she managed to fall asleep and not dream about him. But the next morning when she moved through the living room and glimpsed the white sofa, tears formed within her and her heartbeat slowed to a dangerous level. It would take her a long time to get over this man.

With Bruce it'd been so easy because her love had died years before he was taken from her so violently. The drunk driver who'd plowed into her husband that cold, dark night only put the final touch onto an already dead marriage. She'd grieved for him; for the man he pretended to be before they'd married. She'd cried for the man who'd given her everything, a nice home, an expensive car, a partnership in his law firm—and a separate bedroom as a gift on their first anniversary.

If the business community leaders had known the truth of their union, they would've changed their minds about her.

She jumped a few inches when a loud knock sounded on the front door beside her, punctuated with an even louder threat from Grace.

"I don't feel like trying to explain to Erin why her door is hanging on its hinges," Kate said, "So you might as well come on in."

"Girl, why haven't you answered your phone?"

She didn't get a chance to answer.

"Dear?" Esther's soft hand caressed over her short uncombed hair. "My son did this to you."

"No, I did this to me."

"That boy needs a whipping."

Esther stared hard at her friend. "Even when the boy was young, I didn't whip him."

"Maybe you should've."

My son is hurting as much as she is right now," Esther said looking deep into Kate's eyes. "And no matter what you may think of him, he does care about you. He's just confused."

"No, you don't understand." Looking up at the sad woman, she allowed tears to sneak out of the corners of her eyes. "I made him leave me. I accused him of being something I know he's not."

"He told me."

Startled, Kate asked, "And you're still here, trying to help me?"

"Why wouldn't I be here?"

"I could think of a few reasons." Kate wiped the warm tears from her cheeks. Tired of crying, tired of feeling cold and empty, she forced the wetness back into the depths of her heart. No more tears, she thought. "The first thing is, you don't really know me, and the second is, I called your son a stalker."

"In his fifteenth year," Esther said delicately, "He was stalker-like toward you."

Kate didn't say anything.

"If he had sent those letters, he would've been as bad as that beast threatening Erin." Her tiny fingers settled lightly against her arm. "But he didn't, and I doubt he ever truly planned on sending them at all."

"Then why did he write them?" Kate grabbed at Esther's stilled fingers and trapped the small hand into her larger one. "Why did he decide to...place me on such a high pedestal? I didn't deserve it."

"I don't know why, dear." She squeezed Kate's arm gently. "All I know is that on his fifteenth birthday he went off to the movies alone, and came back a different boy."

"I don't understand how a conniving character like Monica could change a man like Matt."

"The Matt you know is nowhere near the Matt he was then."

"Girl, he was trouble."

"I'm telling the story, Grace."

"Well, then get on with it."

Kate's mood lifted slightly at their friendly exchange, and another stream of tears threatened to fall from her eyes. She would miss these two bickering old ladies.

Both were silent now before Esther said, "Matt had a hard time accepting his father's death. He'd been close to him. They'd done everything together. Matthew—my husband—was killed while protecting a client four mouths before Matt's fifteenth birthday. And during those long months, he was...unruly."

"Troublemaking little pain in the...."

"He started drinking and smoking pot. I put up with that stuff. Always forgiving him. But the hardest thing I'd ever had to do was not bail him out of jail one night. He'd been involved in some misdemeanor crime—I don't remember what it was now—and I decided enough was enough. I asked the police officers to hold him in jail that night. I thought he would never stop hating me for doing that, but I had no choice."

"It was the only choice you had, Esther."

"I know," she said to Grace sadly, "But I can still remember the look on his face when I went to get him the next morning."

"Sometimes, we have to do hard things to help the ones we love," Kate said.

"Yes, it's called tough love."

Bright clear eyes burned into her face, leaving Kate almost breathless at their impact. Matt's eyes, she thought despondently, eyes she'll never see shining for her again.

"Matt was going down a wrong road," Esther continued, "And I needed to do something to stop his descent."

"But on his birthday he went to the movies alone?"

"It surprised me that he wanted to be alone. Grace and I had planned a party for him, inviting some of the better acting kids in the neighborhood."

"He never showed up," Grace added.

"I'll always suspected he'd known about it."

"And he went to see a movie most people would consider a chick flick," Kate whispered, "All alone?"

"I don't think he planned on seeing that particular movie." Esther smiled at the memory. "If I believed in God, I would've said His hand directed my son to enter the wrong room at the multiplex that night."

"Girl, you had the power to make a lot of men take notice back then, and you still do," Grace bellowed. "You've just forgotten how to use it."

"When it comes to men, Grace, I'm as powerless as the next woman." She sighed at the larger woman sitting beside her on the couch. "I have no power over anyone."

"You've power over Esther's boy."

"Over the boy he used to be maybe, but not over the man he is now." If only that were true, she thought. "I've never really had that type of power over any man. Not even my husband."

"Dear, I think you're wrong about that." Esther's look shined bright in Kate's face, a soft warm smile lifting up the corners of her wrinkled mouth. "Maybe your husband left you wanting, but I know you're wrong about my son. He hasn't been with another woman since meeting your friend Erin except for one hasty relationship with Anna."

"That witch," Grace muttered.

Esther ignored her. "Until you came crashing into his life, to play havoc with his heart, he was unhappy."

No, Kate thought.

But could his mother be right?

When you realize you love me, I'll be there, he'd said.

Could it really be the truth?

Chapter Sixteen

Erin arrived home at twenty-five minutes after noon that next Saturday morning, with her new husband in tow. Envy sank into Kate at the first sight of the two together.

She pushed the feeling aside and hugged her oldest friend tight. "Oh, it's so good to see you."

Erin's loud voice and sparkling smile chased all the unwanted emotions from her, and she found her body enfolded in a set of familiar arms. Erin was more than just an old friend; she was like a sister.

"I've missed you too." Her heartfelt statement spoke what Kate's own heart ached to hear. "It's been way too long."

"Hey, it wouldn't have been so long if you'd been here when I arrived." Looking past the heavier woman, she stared at the quiet man. "Now let me see that new husband of yours."

"Hello, Kate."

Staid, she thought. A thin medium height man with an uncomplicated personality stood with one arm around her friend's shoulder.

"Professor, it's good to finally meet you." She smiled at the frown pulling down his tight mouth. "Erin never mentioned your name, but I knew there was someone special in her life."

"You always could read me, couldn't you?" Erin asked.

"You mentioned him once in a letter, in passing," Kate said, glancing past her to the unassuming man, "When she didn't mention you again, I figured something was up."

"It would be more logical if you would've presumed she just didn't have any relationship with me at all."

"You would think that, wouldn't you?" Erin's renewed laughter sailed up one of the deep gashes left by Matt's departure, filling it with friendly warmth. "But Kate could always see past my defenses."

"Dear Erin, to me you're a completely fulfilling best selling book."

Her envy was back.

Kate didn't want to feel this way, yet her heart still hurt as she watched their sweet interactions. Would she ever experience such a love?

The man's voice interrupted her question. "It's time for me to get to the college."

"Yeah, I know." Erin kissed his cheek self-consciously, looking at her quickly from the corner of her eye. "You'll be back by six?"

"It might be a bit later."

Kate looked away, moving to stand by the front window. She heard rather than saw their good-bye embrace.

"It's good to finally meet you, Kate."

Kate turned her head and said, "It's good to meet you too," before twisting back around to stare blindly out the front window.

"So, Kate..." A hand fell on her arm. "Are you ever going to tell me why you turned my recliner?"

"What?" She looked around to spy the puzzlement burning out of her friend's frowning face. "Oh, the chair? I don't really know why I moved it. I think maybe the sun...."

"Oh, really?" A suspicious gleam lingered in her studying eyes before she sank into the corner of the rough sofa and beckoned her to sit beside her. "I suppose you have your reclining chair facing away from its matching couch."

"Look."

"What happened?"

"What do you mean, what happened?"

Erin walked to the window and pulled her to the sofa, settling her down close beside her with a tight grip. As Kate watched her pull the chair to its original position, she swerved her glance back to the window.

"Now that's better." Erin sank into the repositioned chair. "That's more like it."

Memories threatened to override her senses now as she sat at the edge of the sofa.

"Oh, will you just relax, Kate."

"I can't."

"Why in the hell can't you relax in my house?" Sudden knowledge lit in her surprised eyes. "Oh, my Lord, don't tell me. You got lucky on my sofa. I haven't even gotten lucky on it yet."

"Lucky? I wouldn't say that."

"He wasn't any good."

"Oh, he was good." Just the thought of the way he'd loved her sent her heart racing deeper in her chest. "Oh, yes, he was good."

"Then why don't you seem glad about it?"

"He left to go back to San Diego."

"Matt?" A smile broke out on her face; laugher springing loud and clear from an area deep in her throat. "Oh, my Lord, you got together with Matt? Esther must be overjoyed."

"Almost as much as when they found out you married Jack."

"Oh, this is too good."

"Good? Erin, how can you say that?" Shaking her head at her assumption, she said, "I also found out he wrote disgusting fan letters to me when he was fifteen, and kept them."

"Fifteen?"

"He'd obsessed over me for a year, writing me letters and keeping a journal about me. Just like your stalker."

"No, he's not like my stalker." The smile was gone, and Kate wanted to take back her hurtful words. Her friend's renewed fear showed clear in her face. "Matt was a boy who'd just lost his Dad. The bastard who stalked me, who wrote me all those...letters was a grown man. My stalker was a grown man with a beautiful wife and two small children."

"I'm sorry for mentioning him."

Her fear dissolved as quickly as it'd returned. "I'll be all right. I know I'm safe from that man, and so are his wife and children. He'll be in jail for a long while for what he did to that sweet woman. And to me."

"They should never let him see the light of day again."

"Oh, he'll be getting out in two years." Her words seemed to catch in her throat as Kate reached out to touch her arm lightly. "I've been keeping in touch with his wife. I worry more about her than I do about myself."

"Maybe Matt's company can protect her when the time comes."

"Someone from TopNotch all ready does, for free."

"Really?" For some reason this came as a complete surprise to her. Not that he would do something to help another human being, but that he would do it and not tell everyone. "I never heard anything about it."

"Matt's one of the good guys, Kate."

"Is he really?"

"Yeah."

"Then why did he—" Kate cried out as a burning pain lanced through her arm. "That hurt, Erin. What are you trying to do? Break my arm?"

"I will if you don't start talking." When she still didn't speak, Erin squeezed her arm even tighter. "I'm not going to let you go until I find out why my recliner was facing away from my sofa."

"Erin, you're hurting me."

"You made love on my new white sofa with that sexy guy, and…what?"

"I screamed out his name in total ecstasy," she said, jerking her arm away from her painful grip. "Is that what you want to hear?"

She smiled. "It'll do."

"There's nothing more to say. I made a mistake by making love to him."

"You made love not just had sex."

"It's one and the same thing," Kate said quietly.

"I've been with a few men over the years, and I've had a lot of fun." Erin loosened the grip on her arm. Love shined in her almost violent gaze. "But I've never *made love* to a man until I married Jack. Sex is *so* much better when you're in love with the guy. So much better."

Kate didn't want to think of that. Matt was the best lover she'd been with in her life.

"That's why the chair was moved out of the sight of the sofa." Knowledge showed true in her smiling face. "That's why you've been sleeping in my bedroom instead of the guest room."

"How did you know that?"

"You never could make a bed." Erin grinned.

"Oh," Kate said. "I was in the guest room."

"So it wasn't just a one time thing?"

"No," she admitted.

"I always wandered what he'd be like." Her hand reached for her mouth, blush dusting the skin of the cheeks a soft pink. "Or, at least I did until I made love with Jack. Who would've thought someone like him could be so damned good in bed."

Kate smiled at her excitement. "So you really didn't make love to him before you said *I do*?"

"I fell in love with the guy almost the moment I met him." She leaned into her. "But, to be truthful, I thought I would have to settle for a not so great sex life. Was I ever wrong!"

"I'm glad for you." Heaviness fixed deep in her heart, weighing down the broken pieces tight in her lungs. "It was just the opposite for me and Bruce. We'd never made love before we were married, but he always made me ache so bad for it. If nothing else he was a wonderful kisser. I just don't understand...."

"I always thought he was a bastard."

"He wasn't all bad, Erin." The rare times she thought of her deceased husband Kate concentrated only on the good. "He would've given me the world if I'd asked him for it. Somehow he would have found a way."

"Yet he could never give you what you truly needed from him," sadness edged in her friend's tone, "He couldn't give you himself."

"I still don't know how a man who could kiss as well as he did could be so uninspiring in bed." Too talk bad of the dead was wrong, her mom and dad had taught her. She'd tried hard to live by that motto when people asked her about Bruce, about their relationship, about their marriage. "I always thought he was having an affair or that he had to be gay. Yet none of those beliefs were true. He just didn't want me in that way. I don't think he ever wanted any woman in that way."

"Strange man," Erin said.

"Yes." She turned and stared out the big living room window. The sun shone bright in the blue sky, mocking her sad memories. "Oh, why couldn't I find and fall in love with a man like your Jack? Why couldn't I fall in love with a man that set my heart on fire?"

"Matt did that to you, didn't he?"

"With a single touch," she said softly, "He made me melt inside with a single touch."

"Yeah, I like that feeling."

Grief at her loss sprang within her, leaving

unshed tears near the surface of her damp eyes. "I wish things could've been different between us. I wish I could change the way I acted towards him."

"Do you want to know something?" A gentle hand touched her cheek, rubbing away the line of tears falling down her face. "We all—Esther, Grace and I—he was interested in me. We were wrong. I believed it so strongly that I was unsure how to tell him about Jack. I didn't want to hurt him. But when he told me he was happy I'd found someone special I knew he never loved me. Yet he still seemed to have changed according to his mother. And I think I finally figured out why he didn't go back to being a user."

"He used Anna."

"Anna used him, Kate."

"His mom and aunt told me about her."

"She was a bitch." Kate winced as her friend clamped her hand hard around her arm. "I warned him about her, but he didn't listen. She hurt him because he wanted to believe she truly loved him. He told me he hoped she would be different. He even got mad at me when I mentioned 'Three Sisters' to him, implying I was the same as her."

"He accused me of the same thing."

"Really?"

Silence followed her single loaded word before Kate finally said, "I read the article about you signing up to do the series six weeks ago. I called Bill to tell him I wanted to do it, and he verified that it was true."

"Esther didn't want me to tell you." Her smile said it all. "I was hoping you were the reason Matt seemed so different."

"Why would you hope that?"

"Matt and I talked about you a lot." Her wide smile lightened on her face, her hand softened against her lower arm. Erin pulled her back into the soft cushion of the couch. "And when his mom told me he used to have a major crush on Katherine Adams I knew he was still half in love with you."

"No," Kate stared at the window, "Matt was in love with who I used to be."

"And you're still the same."

"No, I'll never be that actress again." Even though that's exactly who she was when she'd made love with the man, she thought. "I don't ever want to be known as Katherine Adams again."

"Bruce made you play that role, Kate, not Matt." Erin said. "It was Bruce who made you separate your past self from your present one. He made you feel like you had to be two different women. If you give Matt a chance he'll be able to help you pull your many personalities back together."

"He doesn't want to do that."

"I believe he does."

"How can you know that?" She twisted sideways to stare hard at her. "Have you been here watching us interact? You weren't here the day we made love on this beautiful new sofa of yours, and you didn't hear me call him a stalker." Sinking back into the sofa, her temper depleted, she added weakly, "I accused him of doing something he will never be able to forgive me for. I've messed everything up."

"So that's it?" Erin said, "You're just going to give up on something good because of a misunderstanding?"

"He'll never forgive me for it," Kate said harshly, "Never."

Chapter Seventeen

Three days later Kate's plane lifted off from the San Diego airport runway, two days after she'd first intended to leave California. Erin had almost convinced her to stay the entire time she'd originally planned; yet she couldn't do it. Too many things reminded her of the mistake she'd made with Matt. It'd been sunny and dry when she'd left Erin's home. Now rain pelted the asphalt around her striking feet as she approached her parked Saturn SL, the dampness of the rain pasting the blue suit jacket and pants tight to her lightly tanned skin.

It was fitting, she thought. She'd worn one of her best work suits on the plane for the return trip because she'd planned on going straight to the office before heading home. No doubt Dana would try to chase her away, try to guilt her into going home sooner than she wanted, but she didn't plan on leaving the office until she was ready to go.

Fitting, she thought again. The California sun had burned hot against her cold, lonely heart, barely warming the surface of it; this cold rain fit her situation so much better.

She unlocked the door and threw her purse into the opposite seat before standing tall and straight next to the dark blue car, ignoring the pouring rain. She stood quiet with her hand on the open door, with her tear-filled face toward the pelting raindrops.

Would she ever get over Matt?

She opened the car door and slide into the seat, looking toward the rain soaked windows. All she could see was his image, the way he measured her

211

when he left her the last time. Her hands gripped the steering wheel hard.

No, she couldn't think of him now.

Driving into the early afternoon traffic, she turned on the main avenue and headed for her office complex a few miles from the airport. A small brick building with the prominent lettering—Williams, Williams, Gay, & Brown—caught her view and a hint of pride entered her mind. And she realized she would never be all alone when she was within those walls. Within that building were people who cared about her, who loved her. She would be all right, no matter what the future had in store for her.

She parked her car in her own spot and stared at the red-brick building for a long time before stepping out of it and moving towards the bright entrance. The door opened at her touch and the scent of fresh flowers assaulted her senses.

Flowers.

Yes, flowers. A big arrangement of pink roses mixed with carnations and bright yellow daisies sat in a lovely clear vase at the side of the receptionist desk.

All her favorite flowers.

"Mrs. Williams?" The young woman looked up from her computer screen. "Dana's going to be angry at you. You're not expected back until the middle of July."

"Really?" She smiled at the woman's shocked expression. "Who sent those beautiful flowers?"

She blushed lightly. "Oh, no, these aren't mine. They're a gift from a client. You remember Mr. Sanderson, don't you?"

"Oh." Disappointment sounded in her voice, even to her own ears. Did she really think he would send her flowers after the way she'd left him? Did she really think he could forgive her so easily? "That was nice of him."

"Kate Williams." A firm voice jerked her head

toward the entrance to the offices. "What are you doing here?"

She turned her head back and leaned over to sniff the flowers before glancing at the surprised younger woman and nodding. "It'll be okay."

"I don't think so," she replied, gently.

"Hello, Dana."

"What in the hell are you doing here?" Dana placed her hands on her ample hips. "You look like you swam from California. Which is where you should still be."

"I don't think that's possible." She stepped past the astonished woman. "Don't get all tensed up. I'm only stopping on my way home from the airport to pick up some work I need."

Dana's hand stopped her forward momentum. "No, you're not going to do that. You're on vacation, and I've been taking care of all your cases just fine. There is nothing you need to pick up from the office."

"So, what you're telling me is to go home?"

Dana's finger touched the side of her head lightly before grinning at her. "I knew all that education wasn't wasted on you."

"I should just fire you."

"Yeah, maybe you should just go ahead and do that."

Laughter warmed the air around Kate. Damn, but she needed this.

"Go home and relax. I have everything under control here," Dana declared.

"You usually do."

"Hey, wait a minute." Kate froze in place as she watched her friend rush into the nearest opened door. She came out and waved a large manila envelope in her hand. A second smaller file sat against the unopened padded envelope. "You received your copy of the revised script and a big package from some guy named Matt. Is this the same hunky guy who runs that security place in San

Diego you *weren't* involved with?

"Yes, that was his name," Kate said.

"Well?" Dana smiled. "Have you been holding out on your best friend?"

Ignoring her question, she only said, "Why would he send me a package?"

"You tell me." Dana glanced down at her hands. "It has 'for your eyes only' on the front of it."

"I hope there's no ticking sounds coming from it."

"I can understand why someone would want to send you a bomb." Dana laughed, but the laughter didn't quite reach the deep shine of her eyes. "But why would Mr. Sexy do it?"

"Let's just say, we didn't part in a very friendly way."

Too quiet, she thought. Her friend was way too quiet for her peace of mind.

"You and this Matt guy. The two of you got to know each other?"

Sadness tore at Kate's heart. "A little bit too well, and way too fast."

"Oh, I'm sorry."

"I'll live."

Dana's arms wrapped around her in a quick hug before she pushed her away and handed her the envelopes. "Maybe you'll find answers in these."

"I doubt it." She accepted both of the objects and tucked them in the crook of her elbow. "I'll check out the script tonight. Did you receive my contract from Bill yet?"

"I'll call as soon as I do."

"Let me know as soon as possible, and I'll come here to read it." Looking down at the thinner envelope, she added, "I need to get that contract signed so we can start filming."

"I don't want to see you anywhere near this building until July tenth."

"July tenth?"

"Yes, that's when your vacation is officially over."

Kate grinned. "All right, I'll only come by long enough to read and sign that contract."

"I'll send it to you."

"Dana?"

"Or better yet, I'll bring it over to your home on my lunch hour."

"I should just fire you.'

"Yeah, you should." She smiled. "But you know you won't."

****

Matt sat in Carlos' old SUV for the longest hour of his life, staring at the well-maintained front yard of the relatively small, inexpensive house. His lady's house. Not the large impressive one she'd shared with that strange husband of hers, but one that suited her so much better.

He still found it hard to believe what he'd learned of Bruce Williams. Rumors aside, he sensed that the man was neither a bastard nor gay. All the information Carlos could dig up on him was that he was a decent man who was faithful to his wife, yet Matt knew deep in his heart the man didn't truly love her.

Not the way she deserved to be loved.

Not the way Matt loved her now, with all his heart. After much soul-searching and anguish, after reading through all those old letters and that year-long journal, he realized the truth. He was meant to be with Kate—and her with him.

The reason why he'd moved from one unsatisfying relationship into another all his life was because his young self had fallen in love with an actress named Katherine Adams. In those letters, especially in the later ones, and in that journal, he'd read the truth of that love. He'd loved Katherine Adams than; he loved Kate Williams now. One and the same.

So simple, yet so complicated.

She had the letters.

Now it was up to her to take the next step, and he'd be near waiting for her to do it.

****

Kate read the contract three times before finally signing her name to it and handing it back to the young receptionist. Not because of any disagreeable conditions in it, but because if she kept her mind focused on the contract she wouldn't need to open the envelope from Matt.

"I'll get this out today," the young woman said, standing just inside the opened front doorway. "Do you need anything else?"

"No." Kate clicked her pen shut, placed the pages back into the business- sized envelope, and handed it to the woman. "Thank you for bringing it over so quickly."

"Dana seemed to think you wanted it signed right away."

She watched the woman close the door behind her, without really seeing her. Her eyes dropped to the envelope for a second before she turned to reach for her cell phone on the stand beside her couch. Bill's assistant answered the phone with a cheerful greeting.

"This is Mrs. Williams. Kate."

"Mrs. Williams, Bill's not in right now." Silence spoke on the line. "It says here he's in Seattle, Washington speaking to a potential financial backer for the series."

"He's in Seattle?" she said, adding, "I live in Seattle."

"You do?"

"Yes." Silence greeted her single word. "He's meeting with someone here, in Seattle, involving 'Three Sisters'?"

"Yes," the woman said, "I think the guy's name is Matt. Hunter, I believe is his last name. He owns

216

a large security firm in this area."

"Matt?"

"Do you know the man?"

Kate shook her head before walking to the sofa where the packet of pages sat. "Could you tell Bill I signed the contract? He should receive it within a few days."

"I'll let him know, Mrs. Williams."

"Thank you." Kate couldn't take her eyes off of the envelope now.

"Maybe you'll see him in Seattle."

"Yes, maybe I will." She hung up the phone without saying good-bye. "Maybe I will."

Why? Had he changed his mind? Did this mean he'd forgiven her?

She needed to read those letters.

No matter what they contained, she needed to read them.

Placing the phone on the hook, she walked over to the large packet and stared at it. She sat down on the couch and slowly opened the top of the envelope with her long nail. A bundle of letters fell out followed by a journal-sized hard covered book. A smaller personal sized letter floated out next, drifting in the breeze of her air conditioner to the floor on the opposite side of the coffee table.

She was suddenly afraid.

What if these letters were like those e-mails?

No, she thought.

She rose up and reached beyond the coffee table for the single letter, and stared at the deep masculine writing on the front of it.

It simply read, "Kate."

Hands shaking, she ripped the seal of the flap apart, slipped out the single sheet of white paper and unfolded it.

Katie,

If you're reading this, you must have received the packet my assistant sent to your office. I don't know if you've looked at the letters yet, but I hope you do.

I took these old letters and journal from my mother's house a week ago. I had every intention of burning them, to get rid of the evidence of my past obsession with you, but I couldn't do it. It took a while for me to realize that you need to read them. You need to understand what I felt for you back then, what I still feel for you now. If you read them as they were originally written, I hope they make sense to you. And I hope they don't disgust you.

I'm in Seattle now, staying at a hotel by the airport. I've got some business to complete here involving your television series. I've decided to be a silent backer. No matter what you decide about me personally, I'll not change my mind about the show. I read the script, and it sounds great.

I'll be staying at the Hilton until the end of the week. If you don't call me, I'll walk away and not bother you again.

But remember this, I love you, Katie. I've always loved you.

Matt

I love you, Katie. I've always loved you, she read over and over again. Warmth of remembrance, from a time not too long past, when he'd whispered those same words sprang to her mind. The day she woke up alone, fearing the worst. He'd kissed her and whispered something she couldn't quite remember until now. *I love you, Katie. I've always loved you.*

Placing the letter gently down to the coffee table, with shaking hands, she picked up the bundle of hand-written letters. This writing was different; weaker, less firm, a boy's writing. She glanced warily at the first word, *Dear Katherine,* before putting the page down and walking toward the window. An older model SUV sat on the opposite side of the street, and she stared at it with interest, but not really seeing it.

Dear Katherine.

Could she stomach these letters? Did she want to know how obsessive the boy was during that terrible time in his life? Could she accept more of the same types of letters as those e-mails?

The still SUV didn't give her any answer.

She walked back to the sofa and sat, forcing her eyes to read. One after another, the sad restlessness of the teenage boy sounded clear, the grief. Tears rolled down her cheeks as she read the sweet, innocent letters, letters nothing at all like those e-mails.

When she reached the final one, her hand froze in mid-air. The last was the one and only one he'd ever sent to her.

She remembered this letter. "Oh, Matt," she whispered. "It's the same one."

Throwing the clipped letters to the sofa, she raced to her bedroom and opened the closet door. A box marked 'From my Past' greeted her eyes as she moved newer boxes around the top shelf and pulled it out. The top went flying across the room a second later, followed by a slue of mementos from her acting life. Her treasured possession lay on the floor around her feet as she gently opened the yellowed letter—the one and only he'd ever sent her, the letter that had touched her heart with such warmth she'd changed her life because of it.

Her marriage to Bruce wasn't the answer she'd been searching for, yet she'd never regretting starting the search. Unfolding the crumpled pages, she carried them back to the living room.

She didn't understand even now why this letter, of all the fan letters she'd received in her life, affected her so much. All she knew was that it had.

Ms. Adams,

You don't know me. I'm just one of your millions of fans.

I'm writing you this letter to let you know that

you've helped me through a hard time in my life. A year ago my father was killed while protecting a woman, and I almost lost me. I started to drink and smoke pot. I ran around with the wrong crowd and caused my mother and aunt and uncle pain. I thought I could never get over the loss of my father. I loved him so much. Then, on my birthday, I went to the movies alone. That day I saw "Midnight Revenge", and I saw you for the first time. That day I started to grow up a bit. Since then I've seen every one of your movies. I've read everything I could find on you.

Rumors are you've met an older man that you're going to marry. And that you're going to give up acting. Rumors are that you're fed up with the way you're treated in Hollywood. I hope you don't give up acting because you're more than just an actress. You're a beautiful person, a caring person, a person who deserves to be happy. But in case you do leave and marry that man, this letter is to tell you thank you. You have made a difference in my life. I'll never be able to say how much.

Your loving fan,
Matt

Kate set the letter on the coffee table and picked up the original. Yes, she thought, they were the same.

Tenderness filled her system as she remembered the day she'd received this. She'd just been turned down for a part in a family comedy, a part she ached to do. She was feeling used, abused, stuck.

Then she'd read this boy's letter. Tears flowed over her cheeks now, the same as they did than. "Oh, Matt."

Fate, she thought with a smile. She watched the letter float from the coffee table to the carpet as she picked up the phone, watched it settle upside down a few feet away.

When the receptionist answered on the other

end, she breathlessly said, "I'd like to be connected to Matthew Hunter's room, please."

"I'll do that for you now."

"Thank you."

Anticipation raced through her system as she waiting to hear his deep bass voice.

"Ma'am, no one's answering at this time."

Was she too late? Did she wait too long to make up her mind?

"Would you like me to leave a message for Mr. Hunter?"

"Yes." *No, she wouldn't believe that.* "Tell him Katie called."

"Katie?"

"Yes," a soft grin stretched across her mouth. "Just Katie."

"I can do that, Ma'am."

A knock on her front door jerked her up and away from the sofa, knowledge singing in her body. Kate knew it was him, somehow she knew.

She wasn't disappointed.

"Matt?" She embraced him hard, dragging him into her brightly lit living room. "I just called your hotel."

"You did?"

"Yes." She stopped at the back of the couch and turned toward him. "I thought you'd left me."

"I'd never leave you."

As he moved passed the couch, a slight breeze lifted up the yellowed old letter and she smiled, softly saying, "Do you believe in fate?"

Emptiness filled his eyes, mixed with something warm and sweet. "Fate?"

"I need *you* to read something now."

He twisted around her and looked at the letters and journal sitting on the couch, the blankness lightening up a bit with hope. "You read the letters?"

"Yes."

"And you're still willing to talk to me?"

221

She stepped closer to him, but didn't touch him. "The real question is—are you willing to talk to me? You haven't accused me of being a stalker."

"You had a right to think that way."

"No, I was wrong." Indicating the letters, she looked at him. "Anna must have sent me those e-mails too. These letters here are nothing like those disgusting things I received in California."

"These may be less descriptive, Katie," he looked away from her, "But that doesn't mean I wasn't a stalker."

"Matt?" She did touch him now, placing her hands on his chest wall. "I was wrong, and I'm sorry."

He didn't say anything. He stared hard at her, with those bare eyes of his, as if reading the truth in her statement. She allowed her eyes to reflect that truth.

Warmth slowly moved past the coldness of his eyes, his despair slowly changing to optimism, as he studied her for long easy minutes. Finally, he said, "You don't have to apologize to me, Katie. I should apologize to you."

"Yes, I agree." Teasing heat flowed from her words, heat Matt didn't seem to hear yet. "You've been a bastard to me since we first met. You've accused me of being far worse than a stalker. I don't know why I put up with you."

He stared long at her, a slow indication of joy forming around the sweetness of his mouth. "I'm sorry."

"Have you changed your mind about me?"

His hand reached out to pull her body tight to him. "I have a feeling you already know the answer to that question."

"Rumor is," caressing her hands over his shoulders, "A certain sexy security firm owner may back a certain television series."

"You talked to the producer?"

"No, to my agent's assistant." When Matt didn't divulge any more information, she said, "Why did you change your mind? You were set against helping to finance the series. I need to know why you changed your mind."

He didn't say anything for so long she thought he wasn't going to answer. Finally, he said, "Anna made me believe in something I thought I never wanted. She made be believe in true love, in family. And when I found her...with that man, I decided true love didn't exist. I was still thinking that way when I saw you at the police station."

"You recognized me, didn't you?"

"Yes, I knew who you were. And I was so sure you were going to do a number on me the way Anna just did. I was sure you were in California for the same reason as Anna."

"I came to visit with Erin. That's all."

"I know that now."

Kate eased away from him, needing to see his face. "And you still don't believe in true love, in family?"

He smiled gently, touching her cheek with the pad of his thumb. "Do you believe in it?"

"Yes." When he didn't answer her after a few second, she said, "Do you believe me now? Do you believe I'm after more from you than just your money?"

He laughed softly. The laughter gave her the answer she needed to hear.

Capturing his face between her hands, she said, "You still haven't told me why you changed your mind about the show."

He placed his hand gently behind her neck and pulled her mouth close to his opened lips. "I fell in love with one of its stars."

Heart racing deep in her chest, breath drying high in her lungs, she said, "Oh, do I know who she is?"

His lips dropped softly to hers, caressing over her skin with sweet delicate strokes. "Earlier, you mentioned something about fate."

"Answer my question." She backed a step, only to have him close the gap. Soon the smoothness of her front door captured her attention, and she sighed against his lowered mouth. "You like trapping me against doors, don't you?"

"I think a certain sexy actress needs to know how deeply I love her."

"Oh?"

"Yes."

"How are you going to show her that?" she whispered. "I can't move."

And he showed her by pulling first one leg than the second up to wrap around his waist, driving her back hard into the wall. His lips captured hers with fiery heat while pressing the hardness of his penis against her wetness. She sighed and wrapped her arms around his neck, rubbing into him.

"Sexy," he whispered, separating their bodies only far enough to pull at the silky white panties beneath her skirt. "I want you."

"Yes." She brushed against his erection as she forced her hand down between them and undid his zipper, pushing his jeans down his hips. And she laughed as one of her legs slipped to the floor. He jerked her panties off of one foot before lifting her leg back up around his waist again. "Oh, yes."

No laughter rang from her lips now, only a loud moan and harsh breathing as he entered her, hard and fast. She whispered his name, time and again, louder and louder, with each of his long, deep strokes. Like a storm roiling in from the mountains, Kate's fulfillment roiled in gently at first, then quickly changed to a fierceness threatening to topple the walls around her.

She screamed out his name as wave after wave of breathtaking pain raced through her system.

"Does that sexy actress realize now how deeply I love her?"

"Oh, Matt."

"Is that a yes?"

Sex, she thought. Did they make love or did they just have sex again?

And what difference did it make?

"Oh, you're a hard one to convince." He lifted her up and walked with her to the couch, tripping over his pants a few times. "I feel pretty damn silly, Katie, with my pants down around my ankles like this."

"Like a teenager again?"

"Sweetie, I'll have you know..." He dropped to the couch and settled her lightly on his lap. "Even as a teen, I never made love to a woman with my pants around my ankles."

"Made love?"

"Yes."

A hard ache fell from her heart, a deep hurt she'd never even known she'd carried with her escaped through her soft sigh at his sweet words. Bruce had done this to her, she thought. He'd emptied her heart with his unloving attitude; with his odd need to keep her unsure and divided. He'd made her separate her many parts; Matt was bringing all those parts of her back together again.

"Sweetie?"

"I love you."

A brilliant smile widened his bruised lips. "And I love you, I've always loved you."

"Was it fate?"

"Yes," he said lightly, fingering her short blonde hair. "I searched my whole life for a woman like Katherine Adams. Some one sexy and alive, warm and real, but I could never find her until I saw you in the police station that day."

"But I'm not that woman anymore."

He gathered her up into his arm; staring into

225

her face with such love it hurt her to see it. "You're all those women. To me, you're every woman."

"Bruce wanted Katherine." Sadness lingered in her at the memory. "I thought he'd be my savoir, but he was only another person wanting me to play a part for him."

"I'm not Bruce."

"But you want me to play a part, don't you?"

Silence rose in the air between them as he studied her. Then he grinned. "Yes, Katie, I do want you to play a part for me."

No, she thought, not you too. "I can't do it again, Matt. I do love you, but I won't separate all that I am for you. I want it all."

"Don't say no until you hear what part I want you to play."

He reached to her feet and took off her shoes. A mere second later her panties sat in a bundle beneath his outstretched legs.

"What are you doing?"

When he started to unbutton her blouse, she slapped his hand away. "I'm not getting naked for you until you tell me what role you want me to play."

"I'm setting the stage."

"By getting me naked?" she asked. "I don't think I want to play any role where I'm naked all the time."

"You won't be naked *all* the time," he said, grinning into her perplexed face. "I'll want you naked when you're in my bed every night, but at other times clothing is optional."

"What in the hell are you talking about?"

"Of course, I'll be naked for you too."

"Matt?"

"I think I'll take you to Hawaii on our honeymoon."

Affection flushed through her, and she felt her lips form into the beginnings of a smile. "I've been to Hawaii. It's not all that special."

His gaze bugged out in faked disbelief.

"And I'm not going to Hawaii with you, on a honeymoon, until you ask me to marry you."

"Will you marry me?" Simple and sweet, direct and to the point, she thought.

"Yes, I'll marry you."

"Will you go to Hawaii with me?"

She pushed him down on the cushion, reaching to his feet to remove his shoes and hanging pants. "Yes, I'll go to Hawaii with you."

"Will you go on a honeymoon with me?"

She laughed, lifting up to allow his hands to play over her nipples as he unbutton her blouse and pulled it apart. "Yes, I'll go on a honeymoon with you."

"And will you lay naked with me every night?"

She held her breath as his fingers rubbed over the expanse of her breasts. "Oh yes, I'll lay naked with you forever."

"Forever?"

"Yes, I'll stay with you forever."

His mouth touched the soft skin between her breasts, and she dragged in a sharp rough breath.

"Will you be my Katie?"

"I'll be anyone you want me to be."

And she meant it.

After all, she was only one person.

Thank you for purchasing this Wild Rose Press
publication. For other wonderful stories of romance,
please visit our on-line bookstore at
www.thewildrosepress.com.

For questions or more information contact us at
info@thewildrosepress.com.

The Wild Rose Press
www.TheWildRosePress.com

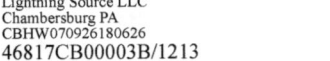